NETFLIX

# STRANGER THINGS

# THE DUSTIN EXPERIMENT

# OTHER TITLES IN THE STRANGER THINGS UNIVERSE

*Runaway Max*

*Rebel Robin*

*Lucas on the Line*

NETFLIX

# STRANGER THINGS

# THE DUSTIN EXPERIMENT

## J. L. D'AMATO

Random House 🏠 New York

Jacket art by Ian Keltie
Jacket art and interior illustrations copyright © 2024 by Netflix, Inc.

Text copyright © 2024 by Netflix, Inc. All rights reserved. Published in the United States by Random House Children's Books, a division of Penguin Random House LLC, New York.

Random House and the colophon are registered trademarks of Penguin Random House LLC. *Stranger Things* and all related titles, characters, and logos are trademarks of Netflix, Inc.

Visit us on the Web! GetUnderlined.com
ReadStrangerThings.com
Educators and librarians, for a variety of teaching tools, visit us at
RHTeachersLibrarians.com

Library of Congress Cataloging-in-Publication Data is available upon request.
ISBN 978-0-593-80850-4 (trade) — ISBN 978-0-593-80851-1 (lib. bdg.) —
ISBN 978-0-593-80852-8 (ebook)

Printed in the United States of America
10 9 8 7 6 5 4 3 2 1
First Edition

To all the kids who proudly claim their title as a nerd, weirdo, or freak. Dustin would be proud.

# PART ONE

# CHAPTER ONE

## FRIDAY, AUGUST 30, 1985

I'm not trying to brag when I say this, but I've had a *lot* of good ideas in my life.

Like the year at science camp when I built a contraption that could grab the chips from the bottom of a Pringles can. (I still think I should patent that one.)

Or that time I told my mom I wanted "pancake lasagna" instead of birthday cake and it was epically delicious.

Not to mention, I was the one to propose the party establish a formal rule of law, both in Dungeons and Dragons and in life, after everything went to hell on the Bloodstone Pass. And those laws have saved our asses more times than I can count.

And then there's the whole thing with me helping save Hawkins and the world from monsters from an alternate dimension on multiple occasions.

I'm just saying, sometimes I astound even myself.

Like now. I've just slammed down a flyer on the lunch table in front of Mike and Lucas, and I'm sure this is my best idea yet.

I'm basically a genius. I'm a mastermind, even. I'm—

"—not really sure, man," Lucas says, voice cutting straight through my self-congratulatory reverie and stabbing me right in the back.

Lucas is munching on almonds casually, as if he hasn't just crushed my dreams. He scans the cafeteria, likely keeping an eye out for Max. She hasn't sat with us for lunch at all in this first week of school, but I know he's still holding out hope. I'm less optimistic.

"What do you *mean* you're not really sure?" I demand.

He shrugs half-heartedly.

"I don't know," says Lucas. "I mean, if we're signing up for Hellfire Club—"

"Of course we're signing up for Hellfire," I say.

"—and, you know, I'm thinking about doing something new, so I don't know how much time I'll have—"

I swipe the flyer off the table and hold it up to illustrate my point.

"But we're science fair *champions*! Does that title mean nothing to you?" I say. "Don't you want to uphold our legacy as *award-winning* scientists?"

Because, as the flyer states, this December, we'll have the opportunity to take our past victories in the Hawkins science fair to the next level with a science and engineering fair in Indianapolis for students across the tristate area.

Mike has been awfully quiet, so I whip toward him. "Come on, Mike, tell him."

He's rushing through next period's Spanish homework, but looks up with an apologetic grimace. I let out a huff before he even speaks. *Et tu, Brute?*

"I don't know. It'd be weird without Will, anyway," Mike says. "Who would make our poster look nice?"

And he's got a point, but—

"You've gotta be kidding me." My eyebrows shoot up as I drop the flyer back to the table, and it flutters down as if it, too, is disappointed. "Both of you? Guys, what is this? What ever happened to the pursuit of knowledge?"

Maybe I'm being *slightly* melodramatic, but it does feel a bit like a betrayal. Science fair was our *thing* in middle school, right up there with Dungeons and Dragons, before our *thing* became fighting those aforementioned interdimensional monsters. And things have been so different already this year, not just with high school starting, but with Will and El gone to California, and Max getting all distant ever since everything went down in the battle of Starcourt, when she'd watched her brother Billy die. I just thought it'd be good to get back to something that brings us together, apart from the imminent threat of death by monster.

"If you want to do it, you should," Lucas says, finally withdrawing from his endless search for Max, to turn his attention toward me. "I just don't want to start off my high school career as . . ." He trails off, not wanting to offend. But I read him loud and clear.

"A nerd?" I guess, eyebrows shooting up again.

Lucas grimaces, and I know I'm right. "I mean, I wouldn't say that. . . ."

"But that's what you *meant,* right?" I ask. "What's wrong with being a nerd? I love being a nerd!"

As if on cue, a blurry mass comes hurtling toward me, and that's all the warning I get before I'm smacked in the head by a stray basketball, pain blooming in the side of my head as I reel back and fall right off my chair.

*"Son of a—"* I'm cursing before I even totally know what's happened, looking around bewildered.

The basketball has landed with a sad plop right on my school lunch tray.

Of course, with all the commotion, half the cafeteria is looking at our table, and at me, sprawled on the ground. They hide tittering, jeering laughter behind their hands, but it still echoes in my ears. Mike and Lucas are both sinking into their seats, trying to be invisible. But I'm out on my ass, and not so lucky.

"Sorry, guys," says some jerk in a green letterman jacket, not sounding apologetic at all as he picks up the ball and wrinkles his nose at the mashed potatoes clinging to the bottom.

"You should really watch where you're throwing that thing," I grumble, against my better judgment perhaps, but my mouth often moves faster than my already-speedy brain. Lucas winces, a hand coming up to cover his face like he doesn't want to be associated with me.

"Maybe you should watch where you put that big head of yours, freak," says the jock.

I can't help but roll my eyes as the guy retreats with the ball to his horde of meatheads. If they're going to throw insults, the least they could do is be a little creative about it. *Freak* is so unoriginal, so uninspired.

I rub the side of my head where I'd been hit and push myself off the ground, dusting off my jeans and smoothing down my T-shirt before dropping back into my seat, where Lucas and Mike are both giving me looks that are half pitying, half commiserating.

"That," Mike says. "*That* is the problem with being a nerd."

Even *I* have to appreciate the comedic timing of it all, though my head is still spinning from the impact.

Someone's voice rises over the temporary quiet of the cafeteria.

"Didn't anyone tell you not to play with your balls in the house, Garroway?"

Dozens of heads whip toward the sound, to find Eddie Munson, standing on a lunch table, calling to the guy who had just hit me with the ball and making a lewd gesture to make it clear basketballs aren't the only balls he's talking about. I watch the interaction with wide eyes and bitten-back laughter.

I know *of* Eddie. Everyone knows of Eddie—he's a hard guy to miss, with the long hair and leather jacket and unapologetically loud presence. He's been a senior for years now, and he leads the Dungeons and Dragons club, Hellfire, and plays guitar in some metal band, and he doesn't seem to give a damn that people hate him for it. I once saw one of the basketball guys try to talk trash to him in the hallway, and Eddie shut him up with a *look*.

He scares people, but to me, he's a legend.

"Shut it, Munson," the jock calls back.

Eddie raises two middle fingers from his fists, aiming them right at the guy with an exaggerated hiss and sticking out his tongue, before hopping off the table and sitting back down, looking quite satisfied with himself.

The jock mutters something under his breath I can only imagine is a string of curse words. But he leaves it at that, miraculously, like he knows better than to mess with Eddie. Like he knows Eddie just doesn't *care*. It's not often I'm rendered speechless, but I'm kind of awestruck.

Slowly, the quiet in the cafeteria lifts as people return to talking.

"That's the guy who runs the Hellfire Club, right?" Mike asks, like he's not sure whether to be terrified or impressed. I can understand that feeling. "He's kind of . . ."

"Epic?" I finish.

"I was going to say *intense*," Mike says.

"Yeah," I say, speechlessness dissipating as I grow energized. "We should try to talk to him. Maybe we can get our names on the sign-up list early."

"Yeah, maybe," Lucas says, thumbing at his ear and avoiding my gaze. My eyes narrow.

"All right, what the hell?" I say, turning to Lucas and pushing aside the tray of food that was desecrated by the basketball. "Where's the enthusiasm? First the science fair, now D&D? Is nothing sacred anymore?"

Lucas huffs, forehead wrinkling. "I'm gonna do Hellfire, okay? I just don't think we need to jump at it."

And the thing is, I know he's once again thinking about the *optics* of it all. Of being associated with someone like Eddie Munson. Of being a weirdo. Of being a *nerd*.

I don't get it, not at all. We've always been the nerds the assholes pick on, and we've always accepted that as the way of the universe. And sure, it'd be nice if people *weren't* bullies, but I thought we were more mature than trying to change ourselves to fit the status quo.

"I hate to break it to you, Lucas," I say, "but we're already nerds. We've *been* nerds. I doubt anything will change that."

The bell rings, signaling the end of lunch.

Lucas frowns, shoulders drooping, and I realize I might have actually hurt him with that one.

He takes a deep breath. "I just"—he sighs—"wanted this year to be different."

He stands up, shouldering his backpack and picking up his lunch tray before I can stutter out a response. He storms out, leaving Mike and me behind. I take a minute before I start gathering my own things. The science fair flyer is splayed on the table, mocking me, so I grab it for good measure.

"I mean, I kind of get it," Mike says quietly as we're walking toward the trash cans, following the steady trickle of students. "The whole—wanting things to be different."

And that's the problem, I guess. Because I hate bullies as much as the next guy, but when it comes down to everything else—I just want things to be the same.

Soon enough, Mike splits off too, heading to his next class, leaving me alone in the diminishing lunchroom crowd flows around me. I look down at the science fair flyer in my hands.

I crumple the paper and drop it in a trash can on my way out.

So much for that idea.

▶

Family Video tends to be empty on weekdays, so when Steve picks Robin up from school for their shift, some days I join them. I like to rifle through the new release shelves or do homework while Steve and Robin trade gossip between interactions with customers, and we all like to judge the film choices of different patrons.

Today, I'm shuffling through the videos with, admittedly, a bit more force than is necessary. The current victim is a children's movie with a cartoon puppet staring back at me.

"It's such a load of garbage!" I say, slamming down another VHS to block the puppet's haunting gaze. "All these moronic bullies who only care about popularity, and girls."

"Yeah, well, welcome to high school." Steve snorts from where he's sitting with his feet kicked up on the counter, flipping through a magazine. It is a timely reminder that, until fairly recently, *Steve* was a bit of a moronic bully who only cared about popularity and girls.

"Yeah, but they've gotten to Lucas, even," I say. "It's like everyone's completely lost their minds, Steve!"

"Can you *please* take your teenage angst out on something *other* than the new release section?" Robin asks, following behind me and meticulously straightening every video I've touched. "I *just* put those out, and it's our most popular section, so if you *have* to mess something up, can you do it to, like, the exercise videos or something?"

"Or the foreign films section. No one ever looks back there," Steve adds, still distracted by the magazine.

"Because they're *heathens* who don't understand that art *transcends* language," Robin says. "Do you know how much you're missing out on because of that perspective?"

"I barely care about movies in English, okay?" Steve says. "And I fell asleep so often in French class, I'm probably conditioned to pass out when I hear it."

"Guys, seriously," I say, interrupting their banter before it devolves further, as it tends to do when it comes to Steve and Robin. "How am I supposed to live like this for *four years*? It's all so primitive. And everyone's acting so different. It's like I'm the only one who kept my sanity."

Steve lowers the magazine he's holding to regard me, unimpressed.

"Look, things change. That's life," he says. "It doesn't have to be a bad thing."

"It *feels* like a bad thing," I say.

Because every recent change *has* been a bad thing, if you ask me. Hopper's death, Will and El leaving. Max growing more and more distant, ever since Billy died. High school, and all of its nonsensical social politics.

"It's one thing for *things* to change. But it feels like the *party* is changing. Like *everyone* is changing, except for me." I pick up a video and turn to Steve with wide eyes. *He-Man and She-Ra: The Secret of the Sword.* "Oh, cool, can I borrow this?"

"Yeah, sure," Steve says, once again engrossed in his magazine, not looking up to even see what movie I'm talking about.

At the same time, Robin says, "No way." She shoots Steve a stern look. "Steve, *please* stop letting your *children* rent movies under the table. I haven't forgotten the *Karate Kid* incident."

"That was *one* time," I say, already tucking the tape into my backpack despite Robin's exasperation. "And it was totally Mike's fault, for the record."

Robin pointedly slides another tape I touched into its

proper position. "I don't care whose fault it was, if you return another tape with the film unraveled like that, and I get fired, and *inevitably* can't get another job in this town, and die of starvation, alone and destitute, I will *haunt* you, Dustin, I mean it."

"*Anyway,*" Steve says, closing the magazine and leaning forward to give me his full attention. "You're growing up. People change. That's normal."

Robin gives up on following me and tidying up in my wake, leaning with a sigh on the counter.

"Yeah, God, do you know how many people that were nice in middle school became total assholes as soon as high school started?" she scoffs. "Like, a not-insignificant amount of people."

This does not cheer me up at all.

"Great," I huff, "so all my friends are going to turn into assholes and leave me alone?"

"It's not impossible, statistically speaking," says Robin. "But you guys are there for each other when it counts, you know? That's what matters."

"Whoa, Robin," Steve muses. "That was almost . . . wise?"

"Don't act so surprised," Robin says. "I'm chock-*full* of wisdom, thank you very much."

"You guys are all changing, sure," Steve says. "But as long as you're changing together . . ."

But what if I don't want to change? What if—

"What if they're changing and I'm *not*?" I ask.

My voice is smaller than I'd like it to be, exposing the petulant whining for what it is: a real, genuine fear. Robin looks displeased and taps the side of her chin thoughtfully.

"Well then, maybe now's the time to try something new," she says. "Do something you wouldn't usually do. Like—watching a foreign film! You might expand your horizons!"

"She's got a point actually, in your situation," Steve says. "You've gotta put yourself out there."

"Like what, joining the basketball team?" I snort at the mere idea. *No thank you.* Can you even imagine me in a basketball jersey?

"Not necessarily," says Robin. "But you could do something else. Join a new club. Audition for the school play. Make new friends. Do something you want to do, for yourself, whether or not Mike or Lucas or anyone wants anything to do with it. Even if it scares you."

It's not like I'm glued to Mike and Lucas. I've never been afraid to do things without them, from going off to science camp and meeting Suzie, to invading hidden Russian bases with Steve and Robin and Erica. But I guess I always saw us heading into high school as a united front. Sticking together, like we always have. It's not like we're totally splitting up, but their easy rejection of the science fair idea still rings in my head as a warning that things have changed, *are* changing.

But I suppose there's that old quote. *Insanity is doing the same thing over and over again and expecting different results.*

And what is science, if not trying new things, keeping an open mind to new questions and possibilities, questioning the norm, and pushing out of your comfort zone? And I'm nothing if not a lover of the scientific method.

"Okay, fine," I agree. "Try new things. How hard can that be?"

# CHAPTER TWO

## TUESDAY, SEPTEMBER 3, 1985

If there's one thing in life I know for sure, it's that any question can be answered with the power of science and purposeful, controlled experimentation.

Like all good experiments, ours starts with an observation: high school is a jungle, the kind that can swallow you right up if you're not careful.

Then there's the hypothesis, posited by Steve and Robin, that trying something new might help me find my place amid all the chaos.

So it's up to me to test the theory.

I head to the big bulletin board littered with flyers for all the different clubs and activities at Hawkins High, promoting themselves ahead of the activities showcase next week. It's kind of intimidating, actually, looking up at all the options. A million potential new clubs, new skills, new friends, new *lives*. But what do I choose?

As far as things that are up my alley, there's a chess club, and a computer science club, and school musical auditions. But I'm not great at chess, and computer science is far less interesting to me than AV technology, which just reminds me again of the way the party used to be, so I scrap those ideas. And I usually only sing with Suzie, so the idea of getting on a stage and singing feels weirdly intimate and exposed, so I count that out too.

Someone walking by bumps into me, too hard to be an accident, shoulder butting into mine and sending me off-balance so I have to catch myself on the wall, almost tearing off a flyer for the drama club. My hat falls off my head and to the ground.

There's not even an attempt at a smart comment this time—which is fine by me, because all of the insults of *freak* and *nerd* and *loser* aren't particularly witty the first time you hear them, let alone the thousandth. All I hear is laughter from the green-jacket-clad jocks as they pass by. None of them even glance at me, let alone help me up.

I take a deep breath to steel myself, biting back a colorful string of curses and insults detailing *exactly* what I think of those jerks. No use getting into trouble or putting a bigger target on my back for nothing. Even if I don't agree with Lucas on much, I get wanting *this* to be different. I pick up my hat and dust it off before tugging it back over my hair.

A copy of the science fair flyer from the other day is staring back at me on the bulletin board, taunting me. I glare at it like it's personally offended me.

"Yeah, yeah," I grumble at it.

I mark this test down as a failure, leaving the bulletin board behind and keeping my head low as I find my way toward homeroom.

That's the thing about science experiments, I guess. You need a controlled setting. And there's no environment *less* controlled than inside the walls of a high school.

▶

Lunch starts the same as it did the first week of school, which is to say, with Mike, Lucas, and me on the outskirts of the cafeteria, clutching our lunch trays and exchanging petrified glances, like we're facing down a horde of demodogs and not debating where to sit.

Except, from there, something different happens.

A guy in a green letterman jacket stands up from his table—the table occupied by the basketball team—and waves right at us. I don't recognize him. He's older, maybe a senior, and tall with dark skin. I look over my shoulder, expecting there to be someone behind us, but there's no one. And then—

"Lucas! Come sit with us!" he calls.

My jaw drops as my head swivels toward Lucas for some

sort of explanation, but I can't think of a single story that would make *this* make sense to me.

Apparently, Lucas can't either, because he just gives us a guilty look before waving back to the guy.

"I'll see you guys later?" he says, apologetic, but not apologetic enough to *not ditch us,* because then he's scurrying off to join the goddamn basketball team for lunch, leaving us in the dust.

I gape after him for a long moment before my jaw clicks shut. "Am I hallucinating right now, or did Lucas just—?"

"You're not hallucinating," Mike says gravely.

Outrage mixes with sinking dread, both weighing heavy in my stomach. Since when is Lucas friends with anyone on the basketball team? For that matter, since when does he have any interest in basketball? Since when does Lucas ditch his friends to fight through the battlegrounds of the cafeteria alone?

"Son of a bitch," I mutter under my breath, scanning the cafeteria with analytical eyes.

The end of the table we'd claimed for ourselves last week is occupied, and the clock is ticking to make a decision, as more and more seats and more and more tables fill up with students. So much movement, so many people, and I don't know where to begin.

"Looking a bit lost there, Weird Al," a voice comes from over my shoulder.

Eddie Munson comes up behind Mike and me, placing a hand on each of our shoulders like we're old friends. I freeze, thoughts vanishing from my head in surprise. *Weird Al?* Oh—

I glance down at my T-shirt, not sure whether to be embarrassed or proud of the tour T-shirt I got when Weird Al came to Indianapolis last year. But Eddie isn't sneering like the jocks would. In fact, he's much less scary than I thought he would be, up close. Besides the long hair and leather jacket, he's just some guy, waiting patiently for me to *say something.*

"Uh" is what I say, which is not the standard of eloquence I like to hold myself to.

"Ah, the wilds of the high school cafeteria," Eddie says, easily filling in the gaps of my brain fart. "The age-old question of where to sit. Am I right? You have to tell me if I'm right."

Mike and I exchange glances, but I'm as lost as he is.

"You're not wrong," Mike says carefully.

"I'm sure you get the gist," says Eddie, waving a hand broadly toward the rest of the room, the many tables steadily filling up with students, pointing out groups as he names them. "Jocks, cheerleaders, band nerds, math nerds, theater nerds, goths—not to be confused with the *punks.* You do *not* want to learn *that* the hard way. And, of course, over there is—"

"The Hellfire Club," I finish for him. I don't mean to geek out about it, but my voice does come out a little reverent. "You run it, right?"

Eddie smirks, pleased, withdrawing his hands from our

shoulders to step in front of us, face to face. "I don't just run it, Weird Al, I *created* it," he says. "Don't tell me you boys are interested in joining?"

"We were thinking about it," Mike says, playing it cool.

*"Hell yes!"* I say, far more enthusiastically. "We've been playing D&D forever. It's so awesome there's a club for it!"

"So, my intuition was correct, then," Eddie says, nodding sagely. "My nerd radar rarely fails me." He gives each of us an appraising look, like we're livestock he's considering investing in. "What do you play?"

It feels like a test, but talking D&D is one of my many special skills.

"Mike's our paladin," I say, gesturing toward him, "and our friend Lucas wants to join too, he's a ranger, and our cleric Will just moved away—"

"And what about you, Weird Al?"

My face heats at the name again.

"I play a bard," I say, pride wavering into uncertainty under Eddie's steely gaze. "And my name is Dustin. Dustin Henderson."

"Well then, Dustin Henderson," says Eddie, nodding, mostly to himself, like he's made up his mind about something. "You guys are welcome to join us for lunch, if you dare."

He jerks a thumb over his shoulder to a table of people in varying amounts of leather, plaid, and denim. They seem like a lively band of misfits, but not in a bad way—quite the opposite, actually. Outside of the party, I've always been the odd one out, from the physical differences of my cleidocranial dysplasia to my extensive nerdy interests. Among misfits, I think I'd fit right in.

Mike catches my eye for another wordless debate, which I don't really understand beyond a series of eyebrow movements that suggest panic. I know he's been having as hard a time with the start of high school as I have, but he's been handling it by holing up in his room with his Nintendo. Which means I need to take initiative for both of us.

"I never turn down a dare," I say.

Eddie gives a self-satisfied grin, claps me on the shoulder again, and leads the way to the table.

I avoid the feeling of eyes on us as we cross the cafeteria. I don't know if I'm seeing things, or if the stream of students really does part like the Red Sea to clear a path for Eddie, until we're at the Hellfire Club table.

"Ladies and gentlemen," Eddie says with a theatrical air about him, regardless of the fact that there are no ladies at the table as far as I can tell. "Allow me to introduce you to Dustin Henderson and Mike—Wheeler, is it?"

"Yep," Mike squeaks out. His older sister, Nancy, and her beloved reputation precede him, as usual.

"These two are potential Hellfire recruits," Eddie explains. "A bard and a paladin."

"That's us," I say with an awkward wave that I immediately regret.

"Sit down, relax, join us," Eddie says, lowering himself into his chair at the center of the table.

Mike and I take the offered seats next to each other and settle in. I can't help but scan the cafeteria. I don't know what I was expecting—as if sitting with the Hellfire Club would cause a seismic shift that alerted everyone nearby that we were big old nerds in need of insulting, pronto—but no one seems to care.

"This is Gareth, and Jeff, and Doug," Eddie introduces, gesturing to each of them in turn. "Our lively band of heroes . . . Gareth the Great is a thief. Jeff plays a druid. And Doug started a new barbarian character a few months ago when *Unearthed Arcana* came out."

They all have an alternative look to them, like Eddie does. Gareth is wearing a plaid flannel with the sleeves ripped off, and has a variety of pins and buttons at his collar and all over his backpack. When I take a peek, I see they're all different band logos, some I've heard of, but most are unfamiliar to me. Doug has a leather jacket over his Hellfire Club baseball tee, and Jeff wears an Iron Maiden T-shirt. It's the kind of stuff that gets you called a freak by people like Jason Carver and his jocks, but these guys just don't seem to care about fitting in. They don't seem to have a problem with being different.

I kind of love it.

I can't help but wonder when I can get my hands on a Hellfire T-shirt of my own.

"Nice. I've been wanting to start a campaign with some of the new rule expansions," Mike is saying to Doug. I kick him under the table, because I know for a *fact* that

Mike is a purist about D&D and thinks the expansions are unnecessary. He ignores me.

Falling into conversation is easy as we all enthuse about our characters, trade stories of past D&D adventures, and wonder about the campaign Eddie's got planned for Hellfire this year. Eddie refuses to reveal anything about it, apart from smiling wickedly in the way Dungeon Masters only do when they have something truly sadistic up their sleeves.

Mike is recounting the time our party got kidnapped by a band of traveling performers, and my bard character had to tell jokes to persuade one of them to help us escape. Mike and Eddie have that DM gene that makes them excellent storytellers, everyone around them leaning in to hear what happens next.

"And he said, 'Beholder? I hardly know 'er!'" Mike says.

The others erupt into laughter, and I feel warmth spread through my chest. Being part of the group is comforting in a way I've been missing, these first few weeks of high school. Sitting with the group doesn't feel scary like I worried it might. It feels like I'm part of something. Like I have a party of adventurers willing to fight at my side, should anything go wrong.

But the thought only makes me wish Lucas were here too. I glance toward the basketball team's table and see Lucas sitting with his new friends, and the table lets out a laugh like they know I'm watching and need to rub it in. I shake it off and return my focus to the Hellfire Club table, where Eddie is fiddling with a Walkman he's produced from his bag, scowls at it like it's just rolled a critical fail.

"What's wrong?" Gareth asks. "You look like someone replaced your Metallica with Madonna or something."

"I'd prefer Madonna to *silence,* the piece of garbage," Eddie says, shaking the Walkman vigorously, tapping at it with the palm of his hand, as if that will do anything. "It was fine yesterday, but it's not playing anything now."

"Let me look at it," I say.

"No, it's fine, I've got this," Eddie says, waving me off to bang the Walkman against the table. I wince on behalf of the innocent technology.

"Seriously, Eddie, give it to me," I insist, thrusting out a hand and wiggling my fingers until he relents.

"Fine," Eddie sighs, exasperated, surrendering the Walkman to me. "See if it listens to *you.*"

I take it gently, as if to tell the poor thing that it's in good hands now and I won't let it get thwacked against the table anymore, if I can help it.

It looks fine on the outside, save for a few scuffs (from the table banging, among other things, I'm sure), so I'll need to look inside. It needs a screwdriver to open, but I'm nothing if not prepared: along with a flashlight, batteries, and an emergency snack, a pocket tool kit is one of the things I keep on my person at all times. (Because being well equipped is *essential* to going on successful adventures, both in D&D and in life.) I dig the kit from my backpack and get to opening up the Walkman.

Undoing the screws is the most time-consuming part.

Once it's opened, exposing all of its inner workings, I immediately see the problem is a sticky wheel and a belt that's come off its track. The dust inside can't be helping either, so I set to work cleaning it the best I can with the limited tools at my disposal. Before long, I'm clicking and screwing pieces back into place.

"Can I see that tape?" I ask, extending a hand to Eddie without looking up, engrossed in the task.

He presses it into my hand. Black Sabbath. I slot it into the tape deck, click it closed, and press play.

Music buzzes to life in the headphones. Eddie takes them and puts them on, breaking into a smile, banging his head along to the music for a few beats.

"Hot damn, Henderson!" Eddie shouts over the music, which blasts so loud in his ears even I can hear the squeal of the guitars. "You're a genius."

"My mother likes to say so," I say with a grin.

"Then this one's for her," Eddie says.

Then he's leaping to his feet, widening his stance, —and rocking out on an air guitar. He gets into it, full-bodied, like he's performing at a sold-out arena and not the school cafeteria. People at nearby tables turn to huff laughs or raise eyebrows or glare before making sly comments to their friends, but Eddie doesn't care about anything but the music. I'm watching, awed by how little he cares about what anyone thinks.

The bell rings, and in an instant, everyone is rushing to clean up and scurry off to their next classes. But Eddie takes the time to finish his solo, so I take the time to watch until the end and applaud, throwing in a few whoops for good measure.

"Oh God, don't encourage him," says Doug. "He'll end up giving us a show at lunch for the rest of the week."

Eddie takes a deep bow with extended arms as Doug, Gareth, and Jeff head out, throwing out *see you later*s and *nice to meet you*s.

"Thanks for joining our motley crew today, gentlemen," Eddie says, leisurely gathering his things even as the cafeteria empties out.

"Yeah, thanks," Mike says. "I'm looking forward to the campaign—but if I'm late to English again, Ms. Beechman is going to kill me."

"She's a stickler," Eddie says, wincing in sympathy. "Godspeed, kid."

He gives a soldier's salute and Mike rushes off. I'm not far off from being late to Latin myself, but I slow myself to match Eddie's pace as we head toward the cafeteria doors.

"Hey, Henderson," Eddie says, stopping short in the doorway to turn to me. I almost walk into him, but steady myself.

"Yeah?" I ask.

He shifts his weight and twists the rings adorning his fingers, and I think this is the first time I've seen Eddie any less than sure of himself.

"You're pretty good with technology and, like, fixing things, yeah?" he asks.

"Sometimes," I say, which is me being more humble than I need to be. "AV stuff, sure, but I dabble in other areas."

"If it's not too much of a pain in the ass, I have this amp that crapped out on me," Eddie says. "And our band's supposed to play at the Hideout next week, but God knows I can't afford a new one. If I lug it to school one day, do you think you could take a look?"

"Oh, yeah," I say. "If I can't fix it, I can figure out what's wrong with it, I'm sure." Through sheer persistence, if nothing else, because there's no way I'm going to let myself disappoint Eddie when he potentially holds the future of my high school experience, and definitely my Hellfire Club experience, in his hands.

"You are a legend, my friend, seriously," Eddie says. "Corroded Coffin and our *legions* of fans will owe you their lives.

"I'll keep that in mind, if I'm ever raising an army," I say, but I sense the sarcasm behind his hyperbole even before he continues.

"It'd be an impressive force of, maybe . . . ten metalhead burnouts and drunken bargoers?" Eddie laughs. "Which sounds like my kind of party. But, hey, I'll bring it tomorrow, yeah?"

I'm already mentally checking out library books on the subject so I can make sure I know what I'm doing, and strategizing on how I can sneak a few books more than the five-at-a-time limit past the librarian.

"Yeah, okay," I say. "I'll see you then."

▶

I come home that night with five books on audio technology and circuitry freshly checked out from the library (and three more smuggled in my bag). Additionally, I picked up a few manuals for recent amp models, some essential tools I don't have already, and a handful of components from Radio Shack, just in case Eddie's amp needs a part replaced tomorrow.

It's completely possible that I'm going a bit overboard, but it's always better to be overprepared than underprepared, if you ask me.

My mom raises her brows from her seat on the couch, Tews the cat curled in her lap and purring as my mom scratches her head absently.

"What's all this, Dusty?" she asks, eyeing my armful of *stuff*.

I'd barely managed to bike home with it all. But Mom's gotten used enough to me going off on random tangents of curiosity to not be too concerned at this point. Most of these little kicks are harmless—and any endeavor that doesn't result in a monster eating our cat is a win in my book.

"I need to become a competent audio technician by tomorrow," I say, dropping a kiss in greeting on the top of her head as I pass by, heading toward my room, where I will camp out for the rest of the night for my curiosity voyage. "I'm helping a friend."

"Oh, how fun!" she says, unfazed. "Try not to cause a power surge, this time, baby?"

I would love to protest that, but it's happened on more than one occasion, and will definitely happen again.

"I make no promises," I say.

My mom sighs, but it's good-natured.

"Well, at the very least, don't electrocute yourself?" she amends.

I'm pretty lucky she's so cool about my endless antics, but I would never say so out loud.

Instead, I say, "I'll try, Mom, thanks!" as I duck into my bedroom. Which I think gets the message across anyway.

# CHAPTER THREE

## WEDNESDAY, SEPTEMBER 4, 1985

Lucas closes his locker and walks off like he hasn't just dropped a bomb on me at eight in the goddamn morning.

"Are you kidding me right now?" I say, immediately stalking after him. "You're actually gonna join the *basketball team*?"

I don't mean to be dramatic, but this betrayal is on par with Saruman joining forces with Sauron, or Lando Calrissian handing the rebels over to the Empire.

"Yeah, I mean, I'm going to try out at least," says Lucas, weaving through the crowds of early-morning loiterers before first bell. I struggle to keep up, but refuse to let him shake me off.

"I've never seen you play basketball in my life," I say. "I don't think I've even seen you *near* a basketball. And me getting smacked in the face with one doesn't count."

Lucas shrugs and keeps his eyes ahead, refusing to look at me. "That's why I'll be practicing with my friend on the team before tryouts in December."

I grab his arm to stop his flight, forcing him to face me, to face his own betrayal. The hallway bustles around us, but I don't care.

"Those guys are assholes, Lucas! Do you really want to hang out with them?" I demand. "Or have you forgotten that *they're* the ones making our lives *hell*?"

Lucas pries his arm out of my grip, but at least he stops fleeing. His eyebrows draw together in desperation, like he wants me to understand what he's saying, but he might as well be speaking Klingon for all the sense it makes to me.

"That's what I'm *saying*! If I do this . . . maybe our lives don't *have* to be hell," he says. "There are people on the team who are *like me,* and they're actually *cool.*"

"*Science* is cool!" I explode. "Dungeons and Dragons is cool! The X-Men are cool! But *basketball*? It's—a pointless ritual glorifying outdated ideals of masculinity."

Lucas crosses his arms over his chest. "Well, it's what I want to do. If you can't make peace with that, then . . . I don't know."

I don't know either. What else can I say? Under all the anger and indignation, mostly I just feel helpless.

"Does Mike know about this? Or Max?" I ask eventually.

"Yes," Lucas sighs, dejected. "They're just as *thrilled* as you are."

I frown, but at least *they* see how ridiculous this is. "What about . . . Are you still going to do Hellfire?"

"Yeah," Lucas says. "Yeah. I want to do *both*."

The bell rings, warning that class starts in five minutes. Lucas adjusts the straps of his backpack over his shoulders with a look on his face like his character has just gotten disabled halfway through a dungeon crawl.

"Well, we'll be sitting with Hellfire at lunch again," I say, turning to go. "If you're not too busy with your new friends to join us."

I leave him standing in the middle of the hallway as students rush in all directions to class. But somehow, it feels like *I'm* the one getting left behind.

▶

After the school day ends, Eddie and I meet up in the AV room that the Hellfire Club uses for meetings. Eddie rushes in, hauling what I assume is the broken amp in one hand, an electric guitar thrown over his shoulder. I've already unpacked my extensive collection of tools from my backpack to create a temporary workstation on the table.

"Hey, man, thanks again for taking a look," Eddie says, setting the amp on the table in front of me and adjusting the guitar over his shoulder. "I know I should probably take it to an actual technician but, you know, money's tight—"

"And my services are free? I see how it is," I tease. I place my hands on the table. "Now, what exactly is the problem?"

Eddie shakes his head and throws his hands up in frustration. "Not a clue, dude. It just kind of gave up and went all quiet and distorted the other day, and it's been like that ever since."

"So it's still turning on, still outputting sound?" I ask. I'm trying hard to sound like I know what I'm doing, even as my nerves prickle at the idea that I might not be cut out for this.

"Yes? But not the way it's supposed to, I guess." He pats the guitar at his side. "I brought my pride and joy here too, if you needed to hear what it's been doing."

I could tell the guitar is his pride and joy without him saying so, with the way he almost caresses it as he twists it around to hold it correctly, showing it off. I don't know enough about guitars to know what makes it special, but I know it makes Eddie look *awesome.*

"I'll take a look inside first," I say, scanning the amp for imperfections. It looks fine externally, a few scrapes that seem to be cosmetic. "But after, it'll be good to play and test it out."

"Whatever you say," Eddie says. "Just try not to electrocute yourself, okay? I don't need that on my conscience."

It takes a few minutes to get everything opened up, and then a few minutes more to get familiarized with the insides. I try to recall the terms I learned last night from binge studying dozens of diagrams of the objects now in front of me. Input. Reverb. Chassis. Capacitors, resistors, transistors.

But the problem is obvious. One of the capacitors is burned and blown out, leaking oozy black discharge. It wouldn't take a rocket scientist to figure out *that* needs replacing.

My nerves settle as I realize I might have actually absorbed enough knowledge to pull this off.

"How'd you learn to do all this, anyway?" Eddie asks, joining me at the table, setting his guitar down with care and letting its long neck rest against the table's edge.

I refuse to admit that all of my amp-specific knowledge is the result of cramming last night in order to impress Eddie. But the answer I give instead is just as true—

"I've always been good at taking things apart, figuring out how things work, putting them back together," I say. "When I was eight, my parents came home to find me with our radio broken up into parts and spread all over the living room. My dad was *pissed,* because it was brand-new, and I'm sure it wasn't cheap, but I promised I'd put it back together. Took me three days, but I managed to get it working again in time for his Sunday night football."

While speaking, I've already removed the broken cap and cleaned out everything the best I can, though I could do it better if I had more materials at my disposal.

"Damn, Henderson," Eddie says. "My dad would have beat my ass."

"Oh, he wanted to," I say. "But my mom? She took one look, and she signed me up for science camp."

She also divorced my dad a few months later, and shortly after that, moved us back to Hawkins where they had both grown up, but that's another story.

Eddie lets out a low, impressed whistle. "Shout-out to Mrs. Henderson, I guess."

"I know it's not cool to admit," I say absently, attention divided by the task at hand. "But she's kind of awesome."

Eddie nods and falls quiet, watching me work.

Luckily, blowing my allowance at Radio Shack paid off, because I have the part that needs replacing, and I install it easily. The multimeter I bought the other day is perfect to troubleshoot the rest, making sure the burst cap isn't the only issue. I fiddle a bit with adding and removing feedback, ultimately adding another capacitor, before I decide that everything's just right. Maybe even better than it had been, but I don't want to be boastful.

I close it up carefully, satisfied, and present the amp to Eddie with wiggling spirit fingers.

*"Voilà,"* I say. "Give it a try."

Eddie hops up, grabbing his guitar, first plugging the amp into the wall outlet, and then plugging the guitar into the amp.

"What should I play?" Eddie asks, poising his fingers over the strings. "Any requests?"

"Uh," I say, floundering for a song request that might make me seem cool and interesting and not totally lame.

But I'm not as much of a music aficionado as Will, or even Max, let alone someone like *Eddie.*

"Come on, what do you like to listen to?" Eddie pushes. "*Besides* Weird Al."

I shrug, noncommittal. "Lots of things, I guess."

"Like?"

He's not accepting *I don't know* as an answer, it seems. I also have the feeling he wouldn't approve of *The Never Ending Story.*

"Uh . . . I like the Talking Heads?" I say, like it's a question. "The Doors?"

"Okay, hell yeah. That's a start. Do you listen to any metal?" he asks, and I shrug sheepishly.

"Not really," I say. "My mom's always been more of a Hall and Oates and the Beatles kind of person."

"But what about *you*?" Eddie asks. "Metallica? Black Sabbath? Motörhead?" He grows more exasperated at my continued blank looks. "Judas Priest? Iron Maiden? Alice Cooper?"

"I mean, I know them all, vaguely . . . ?"

"This isn't the kind of music you can know *vaguely,* like you're hearing it on the radio at the grocery store," Eddie says, shivering dramatically, like even the notion of it is offensive to him. "It's the kind of music you need to get into with your whole body. If you haven't gone full-out, headbanging, jumping around in your room—or, better yet, in a mosh pit—it does *not* count."

I rub the back of my neck, bashful, certain he must

think I'm ridiculously lame. "I can't say I've done that for any of them," I admit.

"We'll fix that," Eddie says solemnly, hand over his heart, with the earnestness of someone making a promise to a person on their deathbed.

"Speaking of fixing things," I say, nodding pointedly to the amp. "Play something, already."

"Yeah, yeah," Eddie says. "Here, I'll bet you know this one, at least."

Slowly, he starts playing a familiar riff. It bursts through the amp with perfect clarity, and I grin, both with pride that my repairs worked, and with recognition at the song.

"'Crazy Train'?" I guess.

"Ozzy *freakin'* Osbourne, man," Eddie says appreciatively, and gets back to speedily picking at the guitar, fingers flying over the strings, the sound filling the room and likely spilling out into the hall, too. But Eddie doesn't seem to notice or care, so I try not to either. When Eddie starts bobbing his head with the song, I do too, and a grin spreads over my face as I get lost in the music.

I end up headbanging so hard my hat falls off my head, and we both laugh, Eddie stopping and putting his guitar gingerly aside as I scoop up the hat.

"Dude, that sounds great," Eddie says. "Better than when I bought it, maybe. What the hell did you do?"

"I'd love to say I never reveal my secrets," I say, "but I just added some negative feedback. Nothing special."

"Sounds like dark magic to me," Eddie says. "I bet you

could doctor up something real nice, if you set your mind to it."

I shrug. "Yeah, I mean . . ." I trail off, mostly because there are dozens of ways you could go about it, dozens of things to change and play with, or things to integrate, like a sampler or playback ability and . . . "You know—that kind of sounds like a good idea for a science project."

"Oh yeah? Are you doing that science fair up in Indy?"

I press my lips together to keep from scowling. I give a half-hearted shrug.

"I don't know, my friends didn't want to do it," I say, starting to clean up the workspace and pack away my stuff, wanting to dismiss the idea and forget it. But my mind is spinning with possibilities. What if the amp could record things, or play things back? What if I optimized everything, upgrading components, testing to measure changes in distortion and signal-to-noise ratios and—

"Do you *have* to have a team?" Eddie asks.

"Not necessarily?" I say, and my heart races at the idea. I can't *really* do this on my own, can I? "I've only ever done it as a team, though, and it's a lot of work."

But that's not it. It's also that it was always the *party's* thing, something we did *together*. And I'm afraid it won't be the same, doing it alone.

"Sounds like now's your chance to try flying solo." Eddie snaps his fingers with a realization. "It's just like Ozzy! He went off on his own after being with Black Sabbath for years, right? He took a break to make *Blizzard of Ozz* on his own, then came back to Black Sabbath. I mean, he did end up kicked out of the band, like, a *year* later?" He waves his hand as if shooing the thought away. "But that's not the point. The point is, who knows if 'Crazy Train' would even exist if Ozzy had been too afraid to do his own thing?"

And maybe Eddie has a point. What if I have the "Crazy Train" of science experiments in my brain, but I let fear stop me from making it reality? What if it's not ditching the party, it's just . . . taking a detour?

"So it's kind of like . . . a side quest?" I ask. That makes it feel less scary—like it's something I can handle on my own, but without having to leave the party.

"Exactly!" Eddie says. "Adventuring parties are important, but some adventures have to happen alone. That doesn't mean it's not worth doing—it just means you get all the experience points for yourself."

And, well, I *have* wanted to try something new, like Robin said. Something that scares me.

I look back to Eddie, who is grinning like he knows he's caught me.

"So the real question is," Eddie says, "are you going to accept this quest?"

▶

"Suzie, do you copy? It's Dustin."

*"I copy, Dusty-bun. You're early today,"* she giggles, pleased.

The sound crackles through the radio and settles over

me like a warm blanket. I sink into my chair, unable to bite back a smile. Suzie is the best girlfriend in the world, and possibly in the whole human history of girlfriends. I always look forward to our radio dates—which we have scheduled twice weekly. She's right that I'm calling a few minutes before our usual time.

"I'm not interrupting anything, am I?" I ask.

*"Not at all! I was just practicing clarinet, but I was about to call you."*

"Good, I couldn't wait to tell you," I say, puffing up my chest even though she can't see me. "I've accepted a noble quest, and will be venturing forth, in pursuit of knowledge and in the name of curiosity."

*"How heroic,"* Suzie says. *"What's the quest? Or is it classified?"*

I tell Suzie absolutely everything, but for her own protection, there's stuff she doesn't know about. Mostly the stuff involving evil alternate dimensions and their associated monsters. So, at this point, she knows that when I start being dramatic, there's a chance it's something I really can't share. That's the magic word, *classified*. If I say that, she knows that means not to pry, that I *really* can't tell her anything. As much as I want to. Maybe one day I'll be able to declassify it. But for now—

"I'm going to do the science fair," I rush out, unable to contain my enthusiasm. "A big one, up in Indianapolis. The one I was telling you about, that Mike and Lucas didn't want to do?"

*"I remember! Did they change their minds?"*

"No, but I did! I've decided that it doesn't matter if they don't want to," I say. "I don't need them! I'm going to do it all by myself."

*"Holy cow, Dusty-bun, that sounds amazing!"* I can hear her smile across the thousands of miles.

"I'm going to make a *super amp,* but with recording and playback functionality so it can be used to make and play music all at once," I enthuse. "It's going to be awesome. Eddie totally inspired me."

*"Eddie is the one from the Dungeons and Dragons club?"*

"He *founded* it," I correct. "And I fixed his amp and his Walkman, so we're basically bonded for life."

*"Wow, Dusty, I'm glad you're making friends,"* Suzie says. *"You sound excited."*

"I am," I realize as I say it. Even though I haven't *told* Suzie about Lucas ditching us at lunch and wanting to try out for the basketball team, I don't feel as totally hopeless as I did when I found out. Maybe Lucas is just on his own side quest. Maybe it doesn't have to be the end of the world.

I'll tell her all about it, I'm sure, and she'll tell me about her chaotic family's latest updates. But first, and most importantly:

"I miss you, Suzie-poo," I say.

*"I miss you more,"* she responds immediately.

I lean my chin on my hand and sigh, and I'll never admit how close I am to swooning. But my talks with Suzie are my favorite parts of the week, every week.

"Not possible," I say. "I miss you infinitely, and nothing's bigger than infinity."

*"Except maybe all the stars in all the universes,"* she says. *"But, Dusty-bun, please tell me you finished reading the next section of* Ender's Game. *"*

We've started our own book club, reading a few chapters at a time and then getting together to talk about them.

"Obviously," I say. "And God, we have *so* much to discuss."

# CHAPTER FOUR

## FRIDAY, SEPTEMBER 6, 1985

I'm so excited about my project and its endless possibilities that it kind of takes over my brain. I research while I'm supposed to be paying attention in class, books on circuitry hidden in my textbooks, scribbling diagrams in the margins of my notebooks. I spend hours in my room fiddling with a voice recorder, an amp, and a soundboard—all purchased by my mother, ever a patron of science, for the project. I'm trying to cobble them together into something new. When I try to sleep at night, I end up imagining the poster and thinking about the presentation I'll make at the fair.

Like now, I'm scribbling a first draft of an introduction for my project—I'm playing with a pun on *ample* but I haven't figured it out yet—while I wait for the others in the AV room for the first Hellfire Club meeting of the year.

I'm especially anxious for Lucas to show up. I barely saw him yesterday or today with him ditching us for the basketball team yet again, but I want to tell him about the science project. I want to tell him how I'm doing it on my own, how we're *both* going on our own side quests and that doesn't have to be a bad thing.

Eddie arrives first, waltzing into the room.

"Hard at work again, Henderson?" he says.

He pats my head through my hat in a gesture that's simultaneously affectionate and patronizing as he passes to drop his DM screen and binder at the head of the table.

"Scientific discovery waits for no one," I say, but I take this as a sign to start packing my work away to dig out my character sheet and notes as well.

Eddie shuffles through cabinets to dig out the game mat and figurines, and we work in companionable silence to get the table set up.

"Hey, man, look," Eddie starts, and I'm immediately running through a million terrible possibilities before he can say anything else. *It's been a good go, but you and your character actually suck and the Hellfire Club would prefer if you exited quietly to your right.*

I wait for him to continue and try not to look too panicked.

He says, "I wanted to thank you for fixing all my shit before." He pats at the pockets of his jacket and jeans before digging through his backpack. "And I figured it's as good an excuse as any to introduce you to the best music has to offer."

At last, he pulls out a cassette and thrusts out his hand in offering.

"W-wait, what?" I stutter, deflating with relief and just as quickly swelling with excitement. Who doesn't love presents? Still, my mother raised me with manners, so I add: "You didn't have to do that."

But I take the tape in my hands gently, like it's the rarest of first-edition comic books, still in its original sleeve.

"Please, it's for my own peace of mind, more than anything," Eddie says, pointedly flippant and casual. "I couldn't sleep at night knowing you've never really listened to metal. That tape has *everything,* okay? The gods of metal. Some hits, a few hidden gems. I couldn't wish a better musical education on my own child."

I study the tape, take in all of its details. It's plain, undecorated, but there's a note in Sharpie, the handwriting rough and tilted:

# Because man cannot live
## on Weird Al alone.
### —Eddie

Warmth surges through me, and I feel light enough that a gust of wind or an exhalation of breath could blow me away. God knows I'd be lost in high school without Eddie and the Hellfire Club, and this just feels like confirmation of that.

Like, I might be a loser, but I'm not alone.

And that's not to mention that Eddie's the coolest person I know, and getting any sort of music education from him feels like studying under a Jedi master or something.

"I'll study it until I know it better than the periodic table," I vow. "Thank you, really."

Eddie waves me off.

"None of that," he says with a pinched expression, like the thanks offends him, or just makes him uncomfortable. "Thank me by listening *properly,* okay? Remember, if you don't headbang to it, it doesn't count."

I can't help but laugh a little, though I know Eddie is dead serious. "Understood," I say.

I tuck the tape into my backpack for later, just as Mike comes in along with Gareth, Jeff, and Doug, all shouting over each other about their characters and enthusing about the campaign.

I watch the door, waiting for Lucas to show up. I know he's been distant and has had other priorities, but he's still one of my best friends, and he promised that he would be doing both Hellfire Club *and* basketball.

But the clock tick, tick, ticks past the time we're supposed to start, and then Eddie's kicking things off with introductions of players and our characters, and we're launching into the story and—

And I don't think Lucas is coming.

I swallow my disappointment, reminding myself that Lucas is busy, that he's trying new things, that he's on his own side quest, and that's all okay. It's not the end of the world. Him skipping one club meeting—even if it's the first and arguably the most important—doesn't have to mean anything.

I try to shake off the worry so I can focus on the campaign. It takes a bit, but I get there, and lose myself in the greatest game of all time.

▶

I'm light and abuzz with excitement from the session, enthusiasm carrying me all the way to Family Video so I can enthuse about it all to Steve. Steve is shelving returns, and Robin is folding a piece of paper into a football at the counter and using a rubber band to line up a shot aimed at Steve's head.

"—totally immersive with music and everything, Eddie's, like, the coolest DM I've ever had," I'm saying.

"Hold on," Steve says, having let me prattle on for a while uninterrupted before he asks. "This is Eddie Munson? As in Eddie 'the Freak' Munson?"

My eyebrows shoot up and defensive anger surges through me.

"Dude, come on, name-calling?" I deadpan, unimpressed. "What are you, a second grader? Or just a generic Neanderthal?"

Robin's paper football launches itself toward Steve, and sadly flutters to the ground a few feet short. Robin sighs as she collects the paper and takes aim again.

Steve rolls his eyes, perhaps at Robin but possibly at me. More likely, at both of us. "I don't mean anything by it," he says. "That's just what everyone calls him!"

"That's not an excuse!" I say.

"Yeah, but, I mean, come on," says Steve. "If the freaky shoe fits . . ."

Robin grimaces at her paper football as she tries to fold it into a more aerodynamic shape. "What happened to keeping an open mind and trying new things?" she asks. "Isn't this exactly what we told him to do?"

"Yes, Robin, exactly!" I say. "Thank you!"

Robin takes aim at Steve once again with her rubber band.

"Can you please stop that?" Steve asks.

"Nope," says Robin, and launches the paper football. It lands at Steve's feet. "Shoot."

"Look, I think your nerdy little science fair thing is awesome, seriously," Steve says, like Robin's paper-based assault is nothing more than a pesky fly, a minor annoyance. "But how much do you actually know about this Eddie guy?"

I know Steve is just being protective, embracing the

whole babysitter thing he's got going for him, but it frustrates me that he doesn't see how much of an inspiration Eddie is to me, and to the other nerds and freaks of Hawkins.

"I know enough!" I say. "I know that he's one of the only people in the whole high school who is looking out for me, and Mike, and the other Hellfire guys. He doesn't care about fitting in, or popularity, or any of that garbage. It's amazing." It's everything I want to be. It's everything I've been trying to be, but never really had a good example of it to look up to. Now I do.

Steve doesn't seem to get it, expression pinched as he slides a copy of Footloose into its proper place.

"I'm just saying, Eddie's got a bad reputation," he says. "And hanging out with him could put a target on your back, you know? Just be careful, is all I mean."

"I don't know, Steve, it sounds to me like you might be jealous," Robin says, collecting the paper football from the floor.

Steve stops in his tracks to glare at her.

"Oh, come on," he says. "Jealous? Of Eddie Munson? Yeah, right."

Robin starts to aim again, and I can't help but pipe up.

"You need to pull down more on the rubber band," I suggest. "Get some more height at the launch."

"Good idea, you little genius," Robin says, and adjusts accordingly, pulling the rubber band lower. When she releases it, the paper football smacks directly into Steve's forehead with a light *thwap!* "Ha! Nice!"

"Just simple physics," I say as she offers a high five and I eagerly accept.

Steve snatches up the paper football before Robin can reclaim it, and Robin and I both boo him for ruining our fun.

"Look, do what you want to do," Steve says, throwing up his hands as if in surrender. "I'm just trying to give some advice, okay? Take it or leave it."

He drops Robin's paper football in the trash.

"Well, I'll leave it, thanks," I say, and start to gather my things.

Because Eddie's mixtape is burning a hole in my backpack. I can't wait to get home and listen to it.

▶

That night, I pass by the piles of books about audio engineering equipment on my desk to slot Eddie's tape into my stereo, closing the tape deck with a satisfying *click* and pushing play.

The music starts. It's thrumming and thick with energy, electric guitar rattling in my bones and drums hitting like sledgehammers, all of it melting together before the singing starts.

I hover over the stereo awkwardly as I listen, nodding along to the beat. I can appreciate that it's good music played by skilled performers, but I'm very aware I'm not listening "properly," as Eddie would probably say.

I can't help it. I don't know how to let myself get into it like that. I've never been a big dancing person, and I'd feel stupid sitting around in my room alone headbanging.

But then I get the sense that Eddie would tell me this music needs to be loud, so I turn the volume up on the stereo and back away.

People dance all the time, so I don't know why I'm making such a big deal out of it. The only time I've really danced was that time at the Snow Ball with Nancy, after being rejected over and over by the girls in my grade. I was nervous then—but this should be easier. I'm alone, with no onlookers to judge me. But like Nancy said back then, I just need to feel the music, feel the rhythm, and start to move to it.

The music thunders around me, and it's new but also familiar in its own strange way. Like, the drums remind me of that time the party stormed an Orcish stronghold and the guards had run to the war drums to sound the alarms. The guitars feel the same kind of electric as Will the Wise's lightning bolt. The vocals make the perfect backing track to an epic battle, swords arcing through the air, battle cries ringing out around me.

That feeling is what gets me to finally move.

Tentatively, I tap my foot to the rhythm of the electric guitar. Then I sway a little bit, and I nod a little bit, and—

And I kind of get what Eddie meant, about listening

with your *body*, because the music feels and sounds different when I'm moving my head to it. My jerky nods get a little more sure of themselves, and I let myself go.

And would you look at that! I'm banging my head!

The music is loud enough to shake the walls, but it's exhilarating, so I turn the volume up even louder and keep going. I shake out my limbs, trying to feel the music and shake off my insecurities all at once. Worries about Lucas and Mike and high school and everything in between fall from my brain.

Before long, I'm jumping around, even breaking out an air guitar when a guitar solo comes on, mimicking Eddie's stance and motions in his lunchroom performance, and—

"Dusty?"

I open my eyes, unaware that they had closed, and my mom is in my doorway with her eyes and mouth forming perfectly round O's. She never comes in without knocking first, but the music must have been so loud I couldn't hear her. I think she probably witnessed a solid minute of my performance before I realized I was being watched, and my face gets so hot I'm sure I look like a tomato.

Sheepishly, I turn the music down.

"Hi," I say.

I give my mom a smile that I hope is charming and not crazed, but I'm panting a little from exertion, so I'm not sure if I succeed.

"What are you doing, Dusty?" she asks, uncertain.

Her expression—blinking rapidly, opening and closing her mouth like a fish, looking away and back again like she's not sure whether she's allowed to look directly at me, until that wavers into a forced smile so that she still seems supportive—it's so perfect I can't help but laugh. Because where would I even begin trying to explain any of this?

I shrug and turn the music back up so I have to shout over it for her to hear me.

I say, "I'm trying new things!"

# PART TWO

# CHAPTER FIVE

## SATURDAY, SEPTEMBER 28, 1985

"Shit."

That's about the only reaction I have time for before the power surges with a crackling *snap*, followed by the sigh of lights turning off, and my room falls to darkness, save for the sliver of afternoon light through the window.

"Dusty?" my mom calls, voice distant.

*"Shit,"* I hiss again, for good measure.

I hastily unplug the amp—I've decided to call it the Bard Box, based off my D&D character, because the idea is that it will have the abilities of a full band of musicians in one box—and leave it on my desk as I yank open the door to my room. The lights in the hall are out too, which means I've not just blown a fuse but also the power in the whole damn house.

Again.

I race downstairs to find my mother in the living room, sitting on the couch with Tews in her lap and the phone in her hand, pressing the keypad to no avail.

"Sorry, Mom," I say with a grimace.

"I was just on the phone with Aunt Kathy about our sisters' weekend," she sighs, then puts the handset back on the hook and turns to me. "Are you okay? You didn't shock yourself again?"

Yes, I accidentally electrocuted myself *once,* last week, when I forgot to discharge the circuit board before I messed with the filter cap, and I'm sure she'll never let me forget it. But, come on, I only singed my hair a *little.*

"I'm fine," I say. "I might have fried the circuit board again, but what else is new?"

My mom's brows draw together and her lips press tight, like she's swallowing a dozen concerns and questions in her attempts to give me space with my process. I get the exasperation—my process doesn't typically require calling the power company twice in a week, but science always takes us to interesting and unexpected places.

"I'll try resetting the breaker," I say, already heading to grab a flashlight to venture down into the cellar.

"Dusty?" my mom calls.

I turn back to face her with a wince, waiting for the scolding I'm sure is inevitable at this point.

She lets out a sigh. "Maybe we should invest in a surge protector?" she suggests, not unkindly.

I sag with relief. Really, my mom's more patient than I deserve, sometimes.

"That's a very good idea, Mom," I say.

# CHAPTER SIX

I've been rambling about circuitry for a good few minutes when I realize Mike has been staring into the abyss of his locker like it's a black hole, and likely hasn't registered a word out of my mouth.

"Hello? Earth to Mike?" I wave my hand in front of his face, and finally he responds, flinching back.

"Sorry," he says.

I was kind of hoping I might still be able to bounce ideas off of Mike and Lucas even if they aren't participating in the fair with me, but as it turns out, that's not an option. Because Mike always zones out if I talk about my project, the Bard Box, for longer than fifteen seconds. And Lucas—

I glance over my shoulder across the hallway to a circle of chattering jocks and cheerleaders, where Lucas is talking with his new friends. The group lets out an obnoxious laugh as one, adding insult to injury, as if they must constantly remind us peasants that they're having a *much* better time than we are.

Mike and I haven't talked to Lucas in a few weeks now. It's not like we set out to avoid him or anything, it's just that he keeps sitting with the basketball team instead of us, and he hasn't bothered coming to the Hellfire Club sessions, so we've stopped trying to invite him.

It sucks, but it seems like it's what Lucas wants. Which really leaves me with Mike, who hasn't proved to be dazzling company as of late.

"All right, what's gotten into you, dude?" I ask. "Am I *that* boring?"

"No, sorry, I just . . . ," Mike says. "Just thinking, I guess."

Not about my science fair project, clearly.

Mike grabs a textbook out of his locker and slams it shut, then blurts out a jumble of words I can barely make out:

"How do you and Suzie do the long-distance thing?"

My eyebrows shoot up. Ever since I proved she actually exists and isn't just imaginary, Mike hasn't seemed all that interested in anything to do with me and Suzie, or our epic Shakespearean romance.

But on second thought, I shouldn't be surprised—the Byers are coming back in a few weeks for all of *one day* to pack up the house before they're gone from Hawkins forever. It's been weighing on my mind, too, but I've had my science fair project to pour all my energy into. All Mike has is his Nintendo.

I tilt my head sideways in thought. "I don't know really, we just *work,* you know? I mean . . . what are you worried about, exactly? I thought you and El were okay?"

"We are!" Mike rushes out. "I mean, there's nothing *wrong.* But it's different, obviously, to go from seeing each other every day to maybe a few times a year."

"Yeah, I mean, it takes extra effort when you don't have proximity as a factor." I think about Suzie, and our little rules and habits in our relationship. "We communicate, I guess, like we're always *honest* with each other," I say. "And we make time for each other. We have scheduled times to talk, and we never miss them. We read and watch a lot of the same things, so we always have something new to talk about."

"Right," Mike says, face tense like he doesn't feel reassured.

"It doesn't have to be the end of the world, Mike, seriously," I say.

"I know," he says. "I know, just . . . Between her and Will . . ."

He stops and shakes his head like he's gotten away from himself, and I can't blame him, because I'm not sure I know what we're talking about anymore.

"What?" I ask.

"It's like, I keep *losing* them," Mike admits, words tumbling from his mouth like they've been waiting to be set free.

And it takes me a minute, but I get what he means.

We thought Will was dead, then we thought El was dead, and now that they're both okay and things are finally calming down—they're leaving again, for good. And we might see them on breaks, but things won't ever be the same.

"You're not really losing them, though," I say. "They'll still be there. You can call, and write letters. California is far, but it's at least got better phone service than the Upside Down."

"Yeah," Mike says, not sounding convinced. "Yeah."

And I get it, I do, the feeling of everything falling apart and being out of your control. I guess I'm just surprised it's taken him this long to catch up with the rest of us.

Just as we're turning away from our lockers to start heading toward class, the circle of jocks starts to move too, and Mike runs straight into one of them, a blond-haired guy, Jason Carver, whom I recognize as one of the team captains.

Jason doesn't hesitate to push Mike until Mike is stumbling backward and sent sprawling to the floor, books flying everywhere, and the crowded hallway bursts into jeering laughter, scattering away from Mike like they're magnets with like poles, repelled by a force they can't explain.

"Watch it, freak," Jason says, and turns to leave, leading the rest of the basketball morons with him.

The bullying hasn't been as horrible as it was during the first week of school, for the most part, but Mike and I are both wearing our Hellfire Club T-shirts for the first time this week after getting them at the last meeting, and clearly, it's put a target on us, functioning as a big old sign that says *FREAK HERE! COME BOTHER ME! I'M A*

*WEIRDO!* I refuse to acknowledge that Steve may have been right about that, because I hate so much that he was.

I rush forward to help Mike gather the books scattered around him, and offer a hand to pull him to his feet. We watch the herd of jocks anxiously as they pass us, and it's then that I see Lucas among the crowd, walking barely a few paces behind Jason. He watches us over his shoulder, and his forehead wrinkles, brows drawing together, like he's sorry, or maybe even guilty. But it doesn't change the fact that he doesn't *do* anything, doesn't *say* anything, just lets it happen, and calls the guy who did it a friend.

The anger and betrayal rise up in me so fast I can't stop myself.

"Really, Lucas?" I ask. "Nothing to say to us?"

As if in slow motion, the herd of jocks stops and turns slowly to face us. Mike gapes at me like, *what the hell did you just do?* To be honest, I'm feeling a similar sentiment as I gulp hard and shrink back against the lockers.

"You have a problem?" Jason barks, emerging from his posse to tower over me. I want so badly to not be intimidated, to look up at him defiantly, to give him crap right back, the way I'm sure Eddie would. But I don't do that. I tuck my chin in defensively and peek at Jason in fleeting glances, like prey afraid to look its predator in the eyes. I try for a smile that I'm sure ends up more of a grimace.

"Nope," I say, voice pitched high. "I'm great. You?"

Like he's asking about my day and not, like, threatening violence against me.

Jason glares at me for a long moment, then jerks his head toward Lucas, who's still watching this all silently instead of telling his so-called friend what a jerkwad he is.

"You know these guys, Sinclair?" Jason asks.

Lucas hesitates, opens and closes his mouth a few times before saying, "I . . . I mean, yeah. Kind of."

*Kind of.* As if years of friendship mean nothing. It's a punch in the gut, a basketball to the head, a glob of spit in my face, all at once.

Jason backs away from me slowly, keeping his eyes on me, *daring* me to try something, just so that he has an excuse to respond in turn. I stay stock-still, so as not to provoke him further.

"Well, watch where you're going," Jason grumbles, glaring at me and Mike in turn before pivoting to rejoin his group and lead them off wherever they're going.

Lucas follows them, and Mike and I watch in silence until they disappear from view. And as Lucas disappears, so does any hope that this is just a side quest for him.

No. This is war.

# CHAPTER SEVEN

## FRIDAY, OCTOBER 11, 1985

"I think Lucas has gone actually, clinically insane," I say as I barge through the doors of Family Video, startling a woman looking through the comedy section so hard she knocks over a cardboard standee for *Planet of the Apes.*

"Oh, for crying out—" Steve starts, hopping over the counter and rushing to the woman to make sure she's okay and fix the standee. "I'm so sorry, ma'am."

He continues apologizing to her, and, inexplicably, to the ape standee, but I beeline to the counter and drop my forehead on it in front of Robin and groan.

"Everything is terrible," I lament.

Robin pats my head uncertainly.

"Uh, there, there?" she says.

"Dustin, I'm sure whatever problem you're having is super important," Steve says as he returns, presumably from apologizing to the woman I startled. "But do you actually *have* to barge in here and cause a whole . . . *fracas* every time you need to complain?"

"I'm not causing a fracas," I grumble, still collapsed on the counter, not ready to face the world again. "And since when do you use the word *fracas,* anyway?"

"I guess I needed a new word to describe the cause of the migraines you give me," Steve says.

"Ha ha," I grate out, sarcastic, and finally lift my face to look at them. I scan the shop, which is now empty. Apparently, I've successfully scared off their only customer. "Now, are you going to give me advice, or just keep blaming me for your medical conditions?"

"What exactly is going on?" Robin asks. "I have a hard enough time keeping up with the trials and tribulations of *this* one's love life"—she jerks a thumb toward Steve—"let alone all of the drama you're wrapped up in."

I settle behind the counter, flopping down on the stool there.

"Lucas has completely ditched us," I say. They already know he's given up on Hellfire Club, and that he doesn't sit with us at lunch. "We've barely talked for weeks now, and today he watched his friends walk all over us and didn't say a goddamn thing! He's lost it! It's like I don't know him at all anymore." My words are spilling out in a flurry. "And like, were we dicks about the basketball thing? *Possibly,* but I still think it was justified, especially now considering he's doing *exactly* what I was worried about, which is letting himself get brainwashed into a giant douchebag!"

I'm out of breath by the time I've gotten it all out. Sometimes, talking things out helps, and you feel better immediately once it's out there, or the problem just feels smaller when it's put into words. This is not one of those times. In fact, it all seems even *more* impossible to solve than it did a minute ago. Except—

"Nope, I don't buy it," Steve says, pivoting to grab a stack of returns and heading toward the shelves to put them back.

My eyes narrow to slits. "You don't *buy* it?" I repeat, springing up to follow him, too much energy to stay still.

"Yeah, it doesn't make sense," Steve says, gesturing with a copy of *Mr. Mom.* "I mean, you guys have been friends for *how* long, and he ditched you? For the sake of popularity? *Lucas?*" He's dismissed it so simply, as if it's possible I have the wrong guy. "I call bullshit."

"Not that what he did doesn't suck," Robin points out, poking her head up over the shelving to add her two cents, "but I think I'm with Steve here. I'd kind of like to hear Lucas's perspective, considering you had your own share of douchiness."

Steve gestures to Robin, a hand wave that says *See? Exactly!* as he puts another movie in its place.

"Great," I sigh. "I come here looking for sympathy, and you're siding with the enemy!"

"It's not the 'the enemy,' dude, it's *Lucas*," says Steve, placing another tape on its shelf. "And besides, you don't come to us for sympathy, you come to us for advice. And my *advice* is to consider that it's possible Lucas is dealing with his own stuff and trying to figure himself out. Like, *beyond* just wanting to be popular."

Robin leans back against a big poster for *Ghostbusters,* which I make note is coming to VHS this month. Too bad the party's such a mess or I'd say we could watch it together. The thought puts a sour taste in my mouth.

"Have you actually tried, like, *talking* to him?" Robin asks. "Without throwing around blame or accusations, I mean? Like, *actually* listening to each other."

"Of course we've tried *talking*," I scoff.

But then, I hesitate, because . . . have we? We've both said a lot of words, but I don't know that either of us were actually *listening* to the other.

"Look, I get that friendships get messy in high school," Robin says. "If you ever want, like, an impartial mediator or something to help you guys talk without killing each other, maybe I can help. I did a few years of band camp in middle school that were so full of drama, I'm basically an expert at navigating the minefields of teenage angst."

I actually don't doubt that, but—

"Doesn't that seem a bit overkill?" I ask. "I don't want to be too dramatic."

"Hate to break it to you, dude, but you passed the line of *too dramatic* a mile back," Steve says.

And he's not wrong, considering this isn't the first time (and won't be the last) that I've swept into the store to complain. The party's fought before, loads of times, but it's never been like *this,* going weeks without speaking. And usually I'm the one mediating for others, not the one needing mediation, so somehow it feels like it's *my* fault it's gotten this bad.

And Robin *is* pretty good at giving advice and staying neutral. Maybe she *could* help.

"Maybe," I say. "I'll think about it."

The door dings as it swings open, letting the October chill make its way into the shop along with a new customer. Steve gives me a pointed look that says I'd *better* think about it, then passes the rest of the stack of returns to Robin before turning to greet the newcomer.

Robin takes up the task of putting movies back in their place, so I take the hint and settle at the counter to put in some work on my project. The Bard Box has evolved at this point into a multifunctional music box, not just an amp but a combination of an amp, a sampler, and a voice recorder, all in one. It might be ambitious, but I'm excited.

And, more than anything, it's comforting. Like, at least I always have this. People may be confusing, but science and amp circuitry, at least, have never let me down.

# CHAPTER EIGHT

10/31/1985

Dear Will,

Happy Halloween! I hope you're having a better one in California than I am in Hawkins.

Sorry, I don't mean to start off our first letters as a total bummer, especially considering we cried enough for a lifetime when you guys came to pack up the house and say goodbye. You probably thought you'd be free from my dramatics for at least a few weeks, but here I am, packaging it up in the mail and sending my angst across the country.

But seriously, as far as Halloweens go, this is the worst one ever. There are parties going on, I'm sure, but we weren't invited. Mike and I weren't, at least. Lucas barely talks to us anymore, so preoccupied with his new cool friends and so obsessed with preparing for basketball tryouts that he's forgotten all about us, as far as I can tell. Max isn't much better, but I don't know what she's up to, beyond avoiding us.

Unfortunately, it seems everything simply falls apart without you, Will the Wise.

I've always thought of Halloween as our holiday. Us, the party, I mean. From dressing up and trick-or-treating to making a party out of going through our candy haul and watching scary movies. But now we're too old to wear costumes, too old to go trick-or-treating, not cool enough for parties, and I hate watching scary movies alone. So here I am, Halloween night, alone, eating candy in my room and writing to you.

On a less depressing note, the science fair project I'm working on is still going well. It's a lot of work, and it's definitely weird not having you and Mike and Lucas to bounce ideas off of, but it's been a fun challenge. Asking questions, seeking answers—the magic of science. Oh, how I love being a nerd.

Are you guys still planning on visiting Hawkins for Christmas?

We all miss you. The party hasn't been the same since you and Et Jane left. It'd be great to see you guys and get everyone together again.

Wishing you all the best from Hawkins!

Your friend,

Dustin

# CHAPTER NINE

## MONDAY, NOVEMBER 11, 1985

I'm trying hard not to be hyperbolic here, but it kind of feels like the world is ending and my life is over.

My mom watches me with nothing but pity and apology from across the kitchen where she's giving Tews a can of wet food. The annoying thing is, she's being too *nice* for me to be mad at her, which means I have to be mad at *me*.

"Dusty, I told you the dates I'd be away ages ago," she's saying.

She did. She *definitely* did, and I let it go in one ear and out the other, because it was months and months away. Until it wasn't—isn't. My mother's weekend trip with her sisters is only a few weeks away now, on the same weekend as the science fair. And while I need to be in Indianapolis, my mother will be in Florida.

"It's just the weekend, and you can call the Wheelers if you need anything—"

I push away the bowl of cornflakes going soggy in front of me. "Can't you celebrate Aunt Kathy's birthday another weekend?"

"If I could reschedule the whole weekend and rebook everyone's flights, honey, I *would,*" she says. "But it's all set in stone. Maybe one of your friends or their parents can help?"

"Shit," I say, then almost say it *again* because I realize I just swore in front of my mom. She gives me a disapproving look, but she's far too used to it at this point to be truly scandalized. "Sorry. It's okay. I'll ask around. I'm sure *somebody* can help."

▶

I call Steve first, that morning, before the bus comes, and ask if he would drive me, but—

"Sorry, dude, no can do," Steve says. "I'm working that day, and after, I finally scored a date with that one chick—"

I still can't comprehend his continued quest for love when Robin is *right there,* but whatever. "Is this the blond one who keeps renting *Grease* over and over?" I ask.

"No, the other one—"

"That girl, Lindsay, with the horror movies?"

"No, dude! Rebekah!"

"Which one is Rebekah?" I ask. I can only keep everyone straight based on which movies they come in to rent, and I don't know how Steve does it.

"The—hot one? I don't know," Steve says. "Point is, I'm busy. My Saturdays are booked out weeks in advance, dude."

"Useless," I sigh. "Fine. I'll ask Eddie."

Steve is probably saying something in protest, because he's skeptical of my new respect for Eddie, but I don't hear his complaints because I'm already hanging up.

I think Eddie is awesome, but it feels ridiculous to ask him for a favor, as if him having taken me and Mike under his wing isn't a big enough favor on its own. I'm half worried that this will be the last straw, that he'll kick me out of the Hellfire Club for daring to ask him, and then I'll *really* have no friends.

And beyond that—Mike was right to say Eddie is a bit *intense*. Just last week, Gareth had to duck out of Hellfire early for a dentist's appointment and Eddie threatened to kill off his character permanently.

So I'm already nervous to ask him when I approach at lunch, only to find him and Jeff nearing a screaming match in the cafeteria over who the better metal guitarist is: Tony Iommi of Black Sabbath or Glenn Tipton of Judas Priest.

I take one look at Eddie, who's nearly crawling over the table to get in Jeff's face as he yells something about Black Sabbath, and I quickly abort mission.

Surely there's someone around here with a functioning car who isn't temporarily insane due to disagreements about music, like Eddie, and isn't in high social demand, like Steve.

So when free period comes around, I head to the music room to find Robin at band practice. She's talking to some red-haired girl between songs, and the band director isn't looking her way, so I take the opportunity to drag her aside to plead my case.

Unlike Steve, she isn't scheduled to work that day, but, according to her rambling and breathless explanation—

"It's not like I have anything better to do on a Saturday than drive an hour and a half to Indianapolis for a science competition I know nothing about," she says, words a mile a minute, "but I don't have a car, and I don't know how to drive, so I'm probably not the *most* viable candidate?"

Which means this is another bust.

Next, I find Nancy in the newspaper room, where she explains to me that she's covering some local pet adoption drive for the paper that day. She wishes me luck, which is nice, but not particularly helpful.

By the end of the day, the situation has made itself clear: Eddie is my only option. I'm sure as hell not going to blow my last chance by approaching him without a plan of action and a persuasive argument at the ready, and certainly not during an explosive metal-related argument. For one, I need to get him alone, when he's not extra intense under the watchful eyes of the basketball team or the rest of the

Hellfire Club. Which means I need to find him in his home territory.

I show up to the Forest Hills trailer park after school, which is a bit of a hike even on my bike, so I'm out of breath by the time I get there. I don't come to this area of town often. I scan the park and its handful of trailers. A woman on one side is hanging laundry on a clothesline, a radio softly playing James Taylor as she does. A few yards over, a couple is camped out on rickety chairs in front of a Winnebago with a cooler between them, smoking cigarettes, sipping from beer bottles, pausing in their chatting to narrow their eyes at me warily. I avert my gaze, settling instead on the junker van I've seen Eddie driving around and the trailer it's parked in front of. Bingo.

I wheel my bike over to Eddie's trailer and drop it in the grass there, looking over my shoulder again before mustering the courage to knock on the door.

It occurs to me, perhaps a few minutes too late, that it might be weird for me to just show up at Eddie's door asking for favors, but I suppose I'm nothing if not audacious.

The door swings open, and Eddie stands there looking mystified.

"Henderson?" He looks over my shoulder as if I could be hiding someone behind me that explains my presence. But there's just me.

"Helloooo," I say, drawing it out as if that will make things less uncomfortable. (Let the record show: it does not.)

Eddie raises his eyebrows for a beat, surprised. Then he

shrugs, adapting quickly with a little jut of his chin like, *this might as well happen,* before stepping back from the door to gesture grandly in invitation.

"Welcome to my domain, I guess," he says.

I step inside, looking around and taking everything in. A suspiciously stained couch, a kitchen counter cluttered with junk, the walls lined with decorative coffee mugs and a collection of trucker hats that makes my own look like child's play. The air smells dank, like cigarettes and something else that I'd guess is weed, but I don't know the smell well enough to be sure. It's all a far cry from the houses I'm used to—mine and Lucas's and Mike's, our parents' suburban dreams—but I'm trying not to see that as a bad thing. Eddie's different from everyone else in a million ways—why would his house be any different?

"I'd offer you something to drink," Eddie says, shutting the door behind me, "but it's basically water or beer, and you're—how old are you again?"

"Fourteen," I say.

"So no beer, probably," he says, leaning back against the counter of the small kitchen space.

"I'm good," I say.

Now that I'm here, all the rehearsed bullet points fall straight out of my head.

"So, what brings you over to this side of the tracks?" Eddie asks.

I swallow hard and steel myself. I can't let my nerves keep me from asking what I came here to ask. *More* than just asking, I have to *convince* Eddie to say yes. He's my only hope.

I muster my best authoritative Dungeon Master's voice.

"Eddie the Banished," I say. Eddie's spine straightens, like the title alone reminds him to carry himself with pride. It encourages me to continue. "A party member—myself, namely—finds himself in need of assistance."

Eddie's mouth quirks toward a smile and he leans in, head tilted, intrigued but not sold. Not yet.

"What kind of assistance?" he asks.

"On the seventh of December," I say, "I need to secure passage to the great city of Indianapolis."

Eddie steeples his fingers and nods sagely. "Is this about your side quest?" he asks.

"It is. It's just—" I throw up my hands and give up on the coded language and theatrics, letting the words tumble out of me in a rush. "I need a ride to the science fair. My mom is going out of town, and everyone I know who can drive is busy, and I've been working on this project for *months,* and now I have no way to get there and . . ."

"And *Eddie* has a functioning car, theoretically," Eddie finishes.

I shrug. "Yeah. And, I thought, if you could drive me—when the science fair is over, the Bard Box is all yours."

"Well," Eddie says, considering. "I've always wanted a Bard Box."

I light up. "Seriously?"

"Nope," he says. "But it does have a nice ring to it."

I deflate, but he's at least considering it. I just need to push him over the edge. I'm not above groveling, but I'm hoping I won't have to.

"Look," I say. "I'm sure you have better things to do, but at this point—" I huff out a defeated laugh. "Help me, Eddie-Wan Kenobi. You're my only hope."

I regret it the second it's out of my mouth.

Eddie says, "First of all, *never* call me that again."

"Done," I say.

"Second of all . . . I have one condition."

My eyes go wide and my heart lurches—it's not a no! It's almost a yes!

"Yes!" I say. "Of course! Anything!"

"Christ, kid—you don't even know what I'm gonna ask."

I roll my eyes. He underestimates how much I need this ride, and besides, it's not like he'd ask for anything weird. "I'll bet money you're gonna ask to be in charge of the road trip music," I guess. "Which is fine, obviously. I'll bring snacks. You can pick me up at, say, eight a.m. the morning of?"

Eddie blinks. His eyes narrow. For a second I think I've pushed too far and insulted him somehow, and he's about to let me have it. But then he barks out a laugh, light with disbelief, like I've surprised him, but pleasantly so.

"Then you have yourself a deal, Henderson," Eddie says.

▶

It's not long before I'm saying goodbye to Eddie and grabbing my bike to wheel it over the grass to the road. That's when I see a familiar figure with a head of red hair across the way dropping a trash bag into a can and then heading back toward a trailer.

"Max?" I call out, uncertain. Maybe it's another girl with red hair and a slight frame. But she turns at the sound of her name and I see her face, clear as day. "Max!"

I lift my hand in an emphatic wave, and watch as she slowly recognizes me and her expression quickly resembles that of a deer in headlights. Like she's been caught.

I pick up my pace and half jog over to her with my bike. She crosses her arms over her chest and refuses to meet my eyes as I draw near. The instinctive smile that took over when I saw her slowly melts off my face.

"Hey," I say again, slowly getting the feeling that running into me was not a welcome surprise. "What are you doing out here?"

Max's face goes tight. I look at the trash can she's just unloaded a bag into, then back at the trailer she was headed toward, and I come to the blindingly obvious conclusion just as she says it.

"I live here now." It's cold, defensive, like she's daring me to say anything about it. I can't help my jaw dropping open, because—

"Why didn't you tell us?" I ask.

I know Max has been distant, and I knew she and her mom were moving after Billy died and his dad left, but I hadn't realized they'd moved *here*. It's not that I'd ever look down on her for living here, but I can't imagine it was an easy change. And it hits me that I have no idea how she feels about it, or about anything, because she doesn't talk to me about any of it. She might not talk to *anyone* about it, I realize.

I feel selfish and stupid suddenly, like I should have noticed, or just *known,* through osmosis, or the sheer power of friendship. It pains me to think *any* of my friends are dealing with such big, terrifying stuff and not talking to me about it. It's almost like we know we can call each other when the evil dimension under our town starts acting up, but not when we're dealing with real stuff.

Grief and trauma and loneliness and *change.* The only monsters worse than the Mind Flayer. But that's exactly the kind of thing friends are supposed to be for. Right? Now it feels like we've made a mess out of everything.

"It's not a big deal." Max shrugs. "Neil left, and this is what we could afford. It's whatever."

Max is putting on a brave, uncaring face, but she's still shrinking into herself, like she'd rather be anywhere in the world but right here with me, her supposed friend who knows nothing about her.

It's kind of humbling. What else might Max be dealing with, or Mike or Lucas, or Will or El for that matter, that I have no idea about? I can answer any question through science, but I haven't bothered asking the important questions to the people I care about the most.

"Are you . . . ," I start, swallowing hard. "I mean, is everything okay?"

Max snorts. "That's a big question."

"Yeah, but, I mean, I'm your friend," I say. "You can talk to me."

It feels like I'm saying this way, *way* too late. But too little, too late has to be better than nothing.

"I'm fine, okay? Really," Max says. "Just . . . promise me you won't tell the others? Especially Lucas."

"Lucas doesn't know?" I ask. I try not to let my shock show on my face this time, but I've never had a good poker face. Even if Max and Lucas have both been distant from *me,* I'd at least thought she and Lucas were doing okay.

"I swear, I'll tell him myself, eventually," Max says, but she's once again refusing to look me in the eye, tugging at the sleeves of her sweatshirt.

"Max . . . ," I start. I don't want to keep secrets from Lucas, not when things between us are shaky enough this year as it is. And more than that, I want to know that Max is talking to *someone.*

"I just . . . ," Max starts, finally looking at me, pleading with me to understand.

And I look at her. *Really* look at her.

Her blue eyes seem duller than normal, lacking the edge of sharpness that makes Max so *Max.* She holds herself like she's injured, hunched over herself.

But more than that—she looks *tired.* She has dark circles

under her eyes. Has she looked this tired for months, and I haven't been paying attention?

"With everything else changing so much, I just want to pretend some things are the same," she says, voice quiet. "Does that make sense?"

It makes way too much sense to me right now. I don't know where I'd even begin explaining that, though.

"Yeah," I say. "That makes a lot of sense, Max."

She gives me a weak smile before turning to head inside.

I watch until she disappears behind the trailer's door before I get on my bike. I point toward home and start pedaling.

I've accomplished my mission, but worry sits heavy in my stomach. And I make a decision. I'm going to take Robin up on her offer to mediate, I'm going to actually *listen,* I'm going to make up with Lucas, and I'm going to bring the party back together, the way it's supposed to be.

How hard can that possibly be?

# CHAPTER TEN

## TUESDAY, NOVEMBER 12, 1985

The next day at lunch, I'm fiddling with the Bard Box, which I've lugged to school to test out. It's coming along nicely now that I've integrated the audio recorder and the soundboard, so it can function as a sampler to play back prerecorded sounds.

Which I use now, for the noble purpose of playing an obnoxious fart sound as Mike sits down at the table with a tray of cafeteria food.

"Whoa, Mike, having stomach problems?" I feign concern, and he glares at me, eyeing the device warily.

"You're going to use that thing for evil, aren't you?" he asks, shaking his head wearily.

I press a button on the soundboard, and the speaker lets out a sad *womp-womp* that I harassed Robin into recording on her trumpet.

"I'll take that as a yes," Mike sighs, and digs into his Tater Tots.

The other Hellfire Club guys haven't arrived yet, which means I have precious little time to talk to Mike alone before they do.

"We're going to Family Video after school on Friday," I say with an authority that I hope he won't question.

"Okay, sure," he says around a mouthful of potato. "You wanna do a movie night?"

"Nope," I say. Then, "Well, maybe, but that's not it. Robin's going to help us make up with Lucas."

Mike's chewing slows, eyes narrowing. "What are you talking about?"

"She's going to mediate," I say. "And we're all gonna talk about our feelings—"

"No way!"

I yell to be heard over his outraged protests. "—and we're not leaving until *everyone* stops being an asshole!"

"Dude, no *way*," Mike repeats. "Why would we need Robin there? And shouldn't *Lucas* be the one apologizing to *us*?"

"That's *exactly* why we need Robin there," I say. "Because we're not seeing both sides."

"I've seen enough," Mike scoffs.

"Come on, man, it's *Lucas*," I say. "Can't we at least hear him out?"

Mike hesitates, swallowing hard, pouting, which is how I know I've almost got him, so I go in for the kill:

"Don't you want your best friend back?"

Eddie, Gareth, Doug, and Jeff roll up to the table, bickering about something, but I don't tear my eyes away from where they're boring a hole into Mike's, like I can Jedi mind trick him into agreeing through sheer force of will.

"Fine," Mike grumbles, finally breaking our staring contest in order to return to his food.

I grin and press another button on the Bard Box, and the sound of a crowd applauding and whistling plays. I recorded that one from the TV while my mom was watching *The Price Is Right*.

Mike rolls his eyes, but I'm too busy feeling triumphant to care.

"What is that thing, Henderson?" Gareth asks, eyeing the Bard Box with suspicion as he and the others take their spots at the table.

"Please don't get him started," Mike says, sounding pained.

"Your science fair project, right?" Eddie says.

"This is far more than just a science project," I say, pushing up to stand so I can better present the device.

"Here we go again," says Mike.

"*This* is the Bard Box," I say, giving it a grand gesture, "an all-in-one music-making box. It's part recording device, part sampler, part amp, *fully* awesome."

I press the button to cue up another *Price Is Right* sound bite of a crowd letting out a collective gasp. I've been practicing my pitch, clearly.

"Are you gonna make music with it?" Jeff asks, raising an unimpressed eyebrow. "Or is its sole purpose slapstick comedy?"

I consider pressing the button that will play a crowd booing, but the fastest way to ruin a gag's charm is to overuse it, so I resist the urge.

"I'm more of a tech guy than a music guy," I say. "But that's why I was wondering if I could bother you guys during a rehearsal one of these days? Maybe take some recordings and run some tests?"

I need to make sure everything works the way it should and see how it handles different frequencies, take some measurements for the data section of my project. Science can't run on fart noises and game shows alone.

"We usually have *closed* rehearsals," Doug says. "We're not just messing around, we're *serious musicians.*"

"And this is a serious experiment!" I defend. The idea that it *isn't* is insulting.

"I think we can make an exception to our tightly run ship for one day," Eddie says. "For the sake of science, or whatever."

"I don't mind." Jeff shrugs.

"Me either," says Gareth.

Doug looks at each of them like this is a great betrayal, and when his glare falls on me, I just offer my most charming smile, blinking up at him innocently, like, *I would never ever be distracting around your Very Serious Band.*

"Fine," Doug says.

I press the button that sounds Robin playing a victorious trumpet fanfare. Doug and Mike groan in unison, but Eddie and Jeff laugh, so I'm counting this as a win.

# CHAPTER ELEVEN

Robin, Mike, Lucas, and I are sitting in a small circle on the floor of Family Video, and none of us will look each other in the eye. Steve is on the other side of the store putting up a new end cap of featured videos, pretending not to eavesdrop, though I'm sure none of us would care even if he sat down to listen.

"So, uh," Robin starts, laughing a little nervously. She has a notebook and pen, which she arranges in her lap. "Thanks for gathering here today."

Mike is the picture of defensiveness, arms crossed over his chest, a scowl on his face. I talked him into joining, but he thinks the whole idea is kind of stupid.

I'm guessing Steve or Robin talked to Lucas, because I *still* haven't really spoken to him in weeks. But he's here now, picking at his cuticles for lack of anything better to do. As I study his face, looking for hints to prove or disprove that theory, I'm almost worried that these few weeks apart have changed him even more. What if he's even more entrenched in jock douchery, or what if he doesn't care enough to fix the mess we've created of our friendship?

I shake off my concerns. This is why we're here. To sort everything out. So I force myself to turn my attention to Robin.

"Okay, so, uh, what are we doing, exactly?" I ask.

"I don't really know, this is my first time doing this," she says. "But, uh, I guess we can start by just saying how we feel? Maybe one at a time, no interruptions?"

No one rushes to volunteer. I glance at Lucas and Mike in turn; they're still avoiding looking at each other or at me. Mike sighs exaggeratedly.

"Okay, fine, I'll start," Mike says. "This whole thing feels like overkill. We don't need an intervention. We just want Lucas to stop being ridiculous."

Lucas moves to interject, but Robin puts out a hand to silence him.

"Okay, new rule?" she says. "Let's not pass judgments or put blame on each other, okay? Focus on your own thoughts and feelings. It can help to start statements with '*I feel.*' Wanna try that again, Mike?"

"Fine," he says. "*I feel* like Lucas is being ridiculous for hanging out with the basketball team when all they do is harass us. *I feel* like it's making him into a total asshole."

I clear my throat and raise my hand. "I also feel that way."

"Well, *I* feel like you guys are being jerks about the whole thing and not even *trying* to understand where I'm coming from," Lucas says.

"Really defeating the purpose of the *I feel* statements, guys," Robin sighs. "Okay, we need to back up. I clearly assumed way too highly of your emotional intelligence. We need to do some trust-building exercises."

"If you tell me we're doing trust falls, I'm leaving," Mike says, and I can't tell whether he's joking or not.

"Listen, *Michael,*" Robin says. "When my cabin in seventh-grade band camp was having an honest-to-God civil war over bathroom usage, and all the girls were taking sides with Becky or Veronica after Becky kissed Jake, who *everyone* knew Veronica had a crush on, I would have thought *nothing* could heal those wounds. But by the end of the summer, we not only had our shit together for the final performance, we were actually *friends.* Do you know what that camp counselor had us do?"

"If I had to take a *guess* . . . ," Mike bites out, sarcastic.

"Trust falls, Wheeler! As well as a few other *trust-building activities* that you numbnuts are going to take *seriously,* capisce?"

She stares each of us down in turn, daring us to say something. I exchange glances with Lucas and Mike, whose expressions match what I'm feeling, which is *what on earth did we get ourselves into?*

"Now stand up. All of you, come on, up!"

I push up to my feet and Lucas and Mike follow suit, Mike grumbling under his breath as he does.

Robin scans the store and, when she sees there are still no customers, waves at Steve. "Steve, help me out here?"

Steve slides over innocently as if he hasn't been eavesdropping the whole time. "With what?" he asks.

*"We,"* Robin says, pointing at her own chest, then at Steve's, "are going to demonstrate a trust fall."

Steve rolls his eyes with a sigh. "Right, sure, okay."

"I'm going to fall backward, and I'm going to *trust* that Steve is going to catch me," Robin says, cutting Steve a look that says *you'd better freaking catch me.*

They assume their positions as the rest of us look on, unimpressed. Robin turns her back to Steve, and Steve holds out his arms uncertainly. Robin closes her eyes and takes a deep breath and then lets herself fall.

Steve catches her under her arms, and Robin lets out a relieved laugh as she hauls herself back up to standing.

"See?" she says, a little breathless. "Easy-peasy. Now let's do you guys. Mike, Dustin, do you want to go first?"

"Do we have a choice?" Mike grumbles.

And, listen, I'm not that enthused about it either, but Mike giving Robin a hard time isn't helpful.

"Come on, dude, let's just get it over with," I say. "Unless you're afraid I'm gonna drop you?"

"I'm not *afraid,* I just don't see how this is gonna help anything," says Mike.

"Well, it certainly can't make things any worse," I say, extending my arms in catching position and wiggling my fingers in invitation. "Come on."

Mike lets out an exaggerated, put-upon sigh, then finally turns around with his back to me. I brace myself to catch him.

"If you *do* let me fall, I swear to God," Mike warns.

"Come *on,*" I say again.

Finally, Mike falls, and I catch him.

Robin and Steve give a polite golf clap.

"Perfect!" says Robin. "See? That wasn't so bad."

Mike straightens up and glowers at Robin, unimpressed. I can't help but laugh, punching him on the shoulder.

"I don't know about you, but I feel closer to you already," I joke.

The rest of the trust falls go similarly—Robin has us do the inverse, with Mike catching me, then calls Lucas up for his turn. Lucas catches Mike, then I catch Lucas, then Lucas catches me, and not one of us drops the other. I don't think any of us would find that funny, and it's a relief that despite Lucas's jerkwad friends, he doesn't seem to have absorbed their cruel streak.

"Would you look at that," Robin says, smiling at us proudly once we've finished. "You guys all have each other's back."

"Is that it?" Lucas asks.

"That, my friends, was part one," says Robin. "You've just progressed to the next level."

I glance at Lucas and we exchange eye rolls, but that's more positive interaction than we've had in weeks, so it's kind of nice. Even if we only end up bonding over the cheesiness of Robin's exercises, I would still consider that a success.

Robin scurries over to the counter and shuffles around in a drawer until she finds a few pads of sticky notes and a couple of pens.

"Here's what we're doing, boys: you guys are going to write down some of your biggest fears on these notes. Then we're gonna put them in"—she glances around, then grabs a promotional popcorn bucket off a shelf and lifts it up—"*this* thing, and we'll shake it up, and I'll read them out anonymously."

Robin passes out the sticky notepads and pens. Mike looks down at his skeptically, and Lucas and I exchange another wary look.

"How is this going to help anything?" Lucas asks.

"Come on, guys, trust the process!" Robin says. "Now get writing. I want at least a few answers from each of you. Surface-level stuff is fine at first, but don't be afraid to dig deep."

With no customers to attend to, Steve leans one hip against the counter and watches as we reluctantly start writing.

Fears. It seems too broad a category, because there's a lot that scares me. I think of the Upside Down, of Demogorgons and demodogs and smoke monsters and flesh monsters. I'm sure Mike and Lucas are thinking the same thing, but I don't want to go there.

I write, *Needles.* Then, *The dentist.* I scribble a few more frivolous ones, then pause. I don't know, I have a feeling Mike isn't going to take this seriously, and I don't want to be the only one being vulnerable. I glance around. Mike is biting his lip and Lucas is scratching the back of his neck as they scribble down on their notes. But ultimately, if there's anyone I trust with my greatest fears, it's these guys. So I write, *Being left behind,* and add all my sticky notes to the popcorn bucket just as Robin claps her hands to bring our attention back to her.

Lucas finishes scribbling and adds his notes to the bucket, and we all sit in awkward silence as Robin shakes the bucket, then starts digging through it, reading our responses silently with a few hums and other thoughtful sounds. My foot taps anxiously as I wait, watching her shuffle the notes into some sort of order.

"I'm going to read out a few of these, okay?" she says. "And I want you guys to say if it resonates with you, if you're afraid of that too. You don't have to say if you're the one who wrote it unless you want to."

I nod, stomach swooping with sudden nerves.

Robin reads the first in the little stack of notes. *"Spiders,"* she says, with a shiver. "Classic."

"I mean, that's basic evolutionary instinct," Mike says. "There are spiders that can paralyze and kill you."

I've never been particularly scared of spiders, or any

creature, really. Maybe something about raising a baby Demogorgon makes you pretty immune to fear of creepy-crawlies. I don't say so, though, not wanting to derail things.

"That was mine," Lucas admits sheepishly.

"It's a good one," Mike says. He and Lucas share a small smile.

"Okay, next one," says Robin. *"Heights."*

"Fair enough," I say. "It's only natural to have a fear of going *splat.*"

It's one of the most common fears, I think. Humans are not made for fall damage.

I'd guess Mike wrote that, only because Lucas has never been afraid of heights, and I know *I* didn't write it. It makes me think back to when we were twelve, when he jumped off the cliff at the quarry, not knowing El would be there to save him. I'd been terrified, thinking I was going to lose a second best friend in a week. I swallow hard at the memory.

"Next up, we have *needles,*" Robin says. This one is mine.

"Oh, that's a good one too," says Lucas.

"Yeah, definitely," says Mike with a grimace.

"That was me," I say with a small wave of my hand.

"And would you look at that! You guys have a lot more in common than you think," Robin says, shuffling through the slips of paper with purpose. "Okay, let's do some more-serious ones."

My heart skips in my chest, nervous for this one to be exposed. But Robin rolls right on:

*"Being left behind,"* she reads.

Mine, again. I focus on my breathing, my heartbeat thumping in my ears, waiting for Lucas or Mike to inevitably crack jokes or poke fun.

They don't. They stay silent, and when I sneak a glance, their heads are hanging low.

"I'll read another," Robin says, voice quiet in the silence. *"Losing my friends."*

I suck in a breath. I didn't write that one, but it resonates, deeply. It's almost the same, in a way, as being afraid of getting left behind.

Still, no one speaks. The silence is unbearably loud, and all I can hear is the heavy sound of Family Video's heating system pumping warmth into the room. Even Steve stills in his sorting of tapes across the room.

Robin shuffles to the next note. Reads, *"Failing the people who need me."*

I can't help but swing my head from Lucas to Mike on either side of me. Lucas looks as stunned as I do, eyes wide like a deer in headlights. Mike is looking down at his lap and blinking rapidly like he might *cry*.

"Do you guys see the pattern here?" Robin asks gently. "You're afraid of the same things. There's more that you guys have in common than what makes you different. And most importantly, you guys *care* about each other."

And she's right, because everything we've been fighting about seems so small in the scheme of our friendship and all the stuff we've been through, from the interpersonal to the interdimensional and everything in between.

I still don't really get Lucas or the whole basketball thing, but maybe that doesn't matter. It certainly doesn't matter enough to keep on not speaking to each other.

"Okay," I say. "I'm done being an idiot if you guys are. Can we just—be friends again? Please?"

"I—" Lucas says. "I thought you guys didn't want me around anymore once I started getting serious about joining the basketball team."

"Of course we want you around," Mike says. "I still don't *get it,* obviously, or *like it,* but we always want you around, man, come on."

Lucas smiles, kind of shaky and uncertain, but that's more than we've gotten out of him for months. It feels good, familiar and warm, and I think this whole thing may have been worth it just for that.

Robin beams at all of us, like a pleased teacher, tucking the notes back into the bucket, save for one, which she dangles between her thumb and index finger.

"This is all super touching, genuinely," Robin says. "But out of curiosity—who wrote *Turbo Teen?*"

Lucas snorts, and Mike and I exchange amused looks, and Steve pops his head up from behind the action movies shelf.

"Oh, that was me," he says, sheepish. "Have you seen that crap? It's haunting."

All of us share a laugh, and it feels good. Right.

And we're . . . not back to the way we used to be, and our friendship is definitely more tentative than it once was. . . . But whatever wound was there, it's not raw and gaping anymore. There's a Band-Aid over it, at least.

And I can only hope it'll heal eventually.

▶

When I get home, there's a letter from Will for me on the kitchen counter. I tear it open, and read:

Nov. 10, 1985

Dear Dustin,

It's great to hear from you! I'm sorry you had such an uneventful Halloween, but I'm sorry to report there wasn't much excitement on my end either, just eating candy and watching TV with El and Jonathan and his friend Argyle. I definitely wasn't invited to any parties.

So far, I haven't made too many new friends here. People are nice, it's just . . . we're the weird kids from Indiana. Sometimes I think it doesn't matter where we go. Like being deemed a freak goes beyond the boundaries of states, or even countries. Like I could go anywhere in the world, and they'd smell it on me.

Now who's being gloomy? It's still early days. I'll find my people, I'm sure.

I do love my art class, though. My art teacher is really cool, and I've been painting a lot more.

Look, I hate to think things between you and Mike and Lucas and Max aren't good. I know our friends can be a bit oblivious sometimes, but they mean well. I think everyone's so hung up on their own stuff, sometimes they forget that everyone's going through it, in some way or another. I think what matters is that they have your back when it counts, and I know they do.

To answer your question, no, we aren't coming down for Christmas. There are still people looking for Jane. And there's a lot of bad memories there for Mom. For all of us.

I do wish I could see you guys, though.

More importantly: you've got to tell me more

about your science fair. What is your project on? What's the fair gonna be like?

All my best,

Will

I can't help but laugh. A step ahead of the rest of us, as always, at least when it comes to feelings. Will the Wise, indeed.

# CHAPTER TWELVE

## WEDNESDAY, NOVEMBER 20, 1985

Even before I pull up to Gareth's house on my bike, I can hear the sounds of Corroded Coffin rehearsing from down the block. I don't know enough about rock and metal to pass judgment, but they seem to be pretty good. They are, at the very least, extremely loud, with the garage doors open wide for anyone to see or hear. It's kind of like wandering into a private concert.

The Bard Box is secured on a cargo rack at the back of my bike, and I pat it to make sure it's okay, then scoop it up in my arms and drop my bike before approaching the garage. Eddie's front and center with his guitar and a microphone, Gareth behind him with a drum kit, Jeff and Doug to either side with a guitar and bass, respectively. I love how they all get *into* the music, and their energy and enthusiasm is contagious, like they really, genuinely love making music together.

Their instruments peter off as they see me approaching, and I try for a wave despite being weighed down by my invention.

"You guys sound great!" I shout over the last trails of guitar and drums as Gareth grabs the cymbals on the drum set to silence them.

"No need for flattery, Henderson," Eddie laughs into the mic. "We've already agreed to be your guinea pigs."

"I'm not flattering, it's a genuine compliment," I say, "and frankly, I'm offended that you think I would stoop to a persuasive technique so devoid of logic."

"Oh, the horrors," Eddie says with a dramatic shiver.

"*I* think we sounded good," Gareth says.

"I don't trust your hearing after so many years behind that kit, dude," says Jeff.

"So what's the deal, then?" Eddie asks me. "We doing science or what?"

"Yes!" I say.

I haul the Bard Box over to the side and put it down on top of one of the other, bigger amps. I pat it proudly the way a car lover might pat a Ferrari.

"I showed you guys the other day, a little bit, how you can record sounds, which get programmed into the soundboard to be played back, kind of like a sampler? But I've also figured out how to make the recorded audio *loop*, and there's the built-in amp, right, so you can kind of lay down sounds and build off of it, and—"

I cut off when I realize they're all looking at me blankly and that I've gone off on a tangent that they do not need to hear.

"Uh, maybe it'd be easier to show you," I say. "Gareth, can you give me a beat? Something simple, anything's fine."

I click the record button as he starts drumming a simple backing beat, and once he gets a few counts in, I stop recording and gesture for Gareth to stop. I assign the sound to one of the buttons on the soundboard and press the button to set it to loop. Suzie helped with some of the programming, but it's not that complex beyond that.

I press the button, and Gareth's drumbeat plays from the attached speaker, looping almost perfectly, with only the slightest hitch between repeats.

"Okay . . . ," Gareth says.

"Just hold on," I say. "Doug, would you add a bass line?"

With a brow raised skeptically, Doug steps forward to let me record an eight count of the bass.

I press the buttons to cue the drumbeat and the bass, and then they're playing together, a tidy little rhythm section.

"And then you kind of layer from there?" I say, suddenly uncertain under their curious eyes. "You could perform live with this as backing, just plug into the amp part of it with your guitar, or you could kind of mix music right on the Bard Box, if you add more sounds, like guitar or vocal riffs or, well, anything, really. . . ."

I trail off, and can't tear my eyes from the Bard Box to

look at any of them, because out of nowhere, I'm terrified they're all going to hate it. That the idea is stupid, not just for the science fair, but for the field of music as a whole, and I've actually insulted them by even bringing it near them.

"I don't know, I mean, the memory's pretty limited, so the recordings can only be so long," I say. "And if you want to loop things you have to time out the counts yourself so it matches up, but maybe I could find a way to integrate a metronome or something—"

But then Eddie's crossing the garage toward me and throwing an arm around my shoulders, his other hand poking at the Bard Box curiously.

"Damn, Henderson, this is pretty sweet," he says.

I perk up under his arm and look at him in surprise.

"Really?" I say.

"Dude, hell yes," Eddie says. "Christ, this is, like, next level. And don't get me wrong, I'm always on the side of live instruments over synthesizers, but this is kind of live, in its own way."

"I can see how it could really fill the sound for a smaller band," Gareth says, leaving his drums to come look at the Bard Box.

"Or even a solo act," Eddie adds.

"Don't be getting any ideas and running off, Munson," Doug grumbles from behind us.

"And you, like, actually *made* this?" Jeff asks, joining the semicircle we're forming around the Bard Box, squatting down to get a closer look.

"The design could be more elegant," I say, putting out the critique before they can. "And a lot of it was just rewiring and reprogramming what's already there from the amp and the recorder and the soundboard. But . . . yeah."

"That's pretty metal, man," Doug says. I puff up my chest, aware that this is an extremely high compliment from him.

"Indeed it is," Eddie agrees. "Now, what exactly do you need from us?"

Pride bursts in my chest at all the praise from some of the most difficult-to-impress people I've ever met. It's both surprising and overwhelming, and I find myself a little flustered even as I put on a confident smile.

"Uh, I'd like to get a few more samples to save, and I need to measure the frequencies and distortion on each of your instruments through the amp?" I say. "It shouldn't take more than a few minutes."

I get to work, and it feels like everything is coming together.

# CHAPTER THIRTEEN

## SATURDAY, NOVEMBER 23, 1985

For the first time in ages, Lucas, Mike, and I come together, huddling in Mike's basement for a horror movie marathon. Max bailed last minute. I haven't seen her since I ran into her at the trailer park, but I'm taking Lucas's presence as a win considering this is our first tentative hangout since we kind of, sort of made up with Robin's help.

Either way, it's almost all of us, sprawled across two couches and under dozens of moth-eaten blankets, eating our weight in popcorn, courtesy of Mrs. Wheeler. We've already gotten through *The Evil Dead,* and we're halfway through *Poltergeist.* We've only survived this long without any of us falling asleep because I have taken it upon myself to throw popcorn at Lucas or Mike whenever one of them gets close to dozing.

"These people are such amateurs," I say, words muffled through a mouth full of popcorn. "I could have clocked this house was haunted on, like, night *one*."

"Yeah, but you *know* it's a horror movie," Lucas says. "They don't have the luxury of being genre-aware."

"Listen, I'm not saying I'd *survive* a horror movie," I say, "I'm just saying I'd last a lot longer than these idiots."

"Technically, I think at this point *all* of us can say we've survived a horror movie," Mike says.

And I know he means it in a lighthearted way, but it kills the mood immediately with the reminder of all the loss and trauma that we just . . . don't talk about. Lucas looks down at his hands, and I'm sure he's thinking about Max, notably absent, as she has been since Billy died. Mike's frowns, and I'm sure he's thinking about El and the powers that went away. I watch both of them, thinking about all the things we can't say.

I search for some way to break the awkward silence, but no words come. Because what is there even to say about flesh monsters killing your friend's douchebag of a brother, or about your friend's superpowered girlfriend losing her abilities after saving the world for the third time?

We pretend to watch the movie so we don't have to acknowledge our problems. I search for something, anything, to break the silence and bring back the enthusiasm we had only a few minutes ago.

"Hey, since we're all here," I say, once the quiet has gone on long enough for the tension to ease from Mike's shoulders, "we should try calling Will and El."

Part of me just wants to show that the party is doing all right after all, considering my last letter to Will painted things as pretty dire. But most of me just likes the idea of all of the party getting to hang out, even if it's across thousands of miles.

The others perk up with interest.

"I'm down," Lucas says. "What time is it in California, anyway?"

"It's a three-hour time difference," Mike says, "so it'd be around five?"

"Perfect," I say, "maybe the phone will be free for once."

Lucas pauses the movie, and I help myself to the basement phone. Mike joins me and calls out the phone number as I dial. Lucas joins us, and we circle around the phone as it rings. I turn up the volume as loud as it goes so that everyone can hear (albeit with some distortion) if I hold the receiver in the middle of our little circle.

I'm half expecting Joyce or Jonathan to answer, but then—

*"Hello?"* Despite the crackling of the phone, it's undeniably Will's voice.

We all respond immediately and rambunctiously—

"Byers!" Lucas shouts.

At the same time, I exclaim, "Will the Wise!"

Mike murmurs his own, quieter "Hey, Will."

Will huffs a laugh. *"Wow, the whole party!"* I can hear the smile in his voice. *"It's so good to hear you guys. Hold on—let me let, um,* Jane, *say hi—"*

I still can't get the hang of calling El *Jane,* but our calls could be monitored, and we'll all do whatever we can to protect El. There's a quiet rustle as the phone presumably exchanges hands.

El speaks, voice tentative but warm. *"Hi,"* she says.

"Hey, Jane!" I say. "Always the chatterbox."

"We miss you," Lucas adds, leaning in so the receiver will pick up his voice.

"We're in Mike's basement watching scary movies," I announce. "What are you guys up to?"

*"Homework,"* Will laughs. *"Sorry, I wish I could say something more exciting."*

"So, you haven't taken up surfing yet?" I ask. "Adopted a Valley Girl accent?"

*"Not yet,"* Will says, good-natured as ever.

Mike pries the phone from my hands. "So you haven't gone completely local, then?"

*"You can take the Byers out of Hawkins . . . ,"* Will says, leaving the rest of the idiom unspoken.

*"We have become fans of their breakfast burritos, however,"* El adds.

There's a beat where we're all just grinning in a circle around the phone, then, *"I wish we could be there, seriously,"* Will says, quiet. *"I miss you guys. We both do."*

*"But things are okay here,"* El says. Then, after a pause, she adds, *"Things are* good."

Will is a bit more hesitant when he says, *"Yeah. Yeah, I mean we're doing all right."*

I can't help but notice that El doesn't have much to say in general, and that Mike doesn't have much to say to El. I knew Mike was nervous about doing the long-distance thing, but sheesh. Not everyone can be me and Suzie, I guess. Or maybe they talk so much they just don't have anything to say right now. I don't really know.

*"How's the D&D club?"* Will asks. *"And, Lucas, when are your basketball tryouts again?"*

"December second," Lucas answers. "I've been practicing hard, but we'll see how it goes."

I roll my eyes at the reminder of Lucas's insane endeavor, then wonder if I should feel guilty for not having known that myself. For not having bothered to ask.

"Hellfire's awesome," Mike says. "Eddie's a legend as a DM."

"A cruel, twisted, *ruthless* DM," I add, "but yeah, definitely legendary."

"Maybe next time you come visit he'd let you sit in for a session," Mike says.

*"Maybe, that'd be cool,"* Will laughs. *"What else, what about the science fair? How's the project coming along?"*

I light up and grab at the phone, but Mike's grip is so tight that I can't tug it toward me.

"Oh God, don't get him started," Mike says. "If I hear any more about circuits and audio recording I'm going to lose it."

*"Well, I think it's awesome,"* Will says, and I can hear

genuine enthusiasm in his voice. *"It's really cool to do it all by yourself."*

"Thanks, man," I say, and bite back the tangent about circuitry that's on the tip of my tongue, for Mike's sake.

"Oh, I've been meaning to ask," Mike says, not to the phone, but to me. "Like, I don't know if the big fancy showcase will let you bring guests? But if you want, maybe we could come and support you, you know?"

"Oh, that's a good idea," says Lucas. "I know you really wanted to do it with the party, the least we can do is cheer you on."

I can't help but be surprised—both Lucas and Mike seemed so uninterested in the science fair from the get-go, I was sure they'd want nothing to do with it and would just let me do my own thing alone. But even if I'm doing the project alone, it'd mean a lot to have them there to see it. It might be a solo quest, but that doesn't mean I can't get help from some allies.

"Yeah," I say. "Yeah, that'd be cool."

*"It's nice to hear your voices,"* El says.

I can't bite back my smile, overwhelmed by fondness for my friends. I'd been so worried that the party was falling apart, but maybe the anxiety was unnecessary. Because here we are, as together as we can be, for the first time in a while, and it feels like everything will be okay.

"You guys too," I say, and I really, really mean it.

# CHAPTER FOURTEEN

## TUESDAY, DECEMBER 3, 1985

Somehow, things are actually coming together.

The Bard Box is not just functioning well, it's appropriately *epic,* leaving me to focus on putting together my presentation and poster, and preparing for questions from the judges.

We're in Mike's basement after school, theoretically to study for a history test tomorrow. I've not only given up on that to work on my project, I've also roped Mike in to help read over the text components going on the board, because he's always been better at English than I am.

He's frowning, hunched over the papers I've given him, scribbling circles and underlining with a pen. I wait, antsy, shifting in my seat, as if he will finish reading and decide the whole draft needs to go in the trash only days before the fair. But after an excruciating few minutes, he neatly shuffles the papers, tapping them together on the desk to straighten them, and offers them back to me.

"There were a few grammatical things I pointed out," he says. "But the substance is really solid." His eyebrows lift like he's actually impressed, which pleases me more than I want to admit.

I accept the papers and shuffle through them, noting his edits, which are all things I never would have caught on my own.

" 'Really solid,' " I repeat, proud. "That's basically a rave review."

Mike's been distant lately, or distracted, or something. At the very least, he's been uninterested in my project until now, so the small note of praise is encouraging.

"It was always the question-and-answer part of the presentation that used to get me," Lucas says, using a pencil as a bookmark and closing his textbook on it. "We'd think we were well prepared and Mr. Clarke would hit us with something completely out of left field."

"I think I can improvise my way out of it," I say, but I'm suddenly wondering if I should have prepared for more outside-the-box questions.

"I could grill you about your project," Lucas offers. "Like a practice interview."

I glance toward Mike, who has ditched the table to

collapse on the couch, history book forgotten.

"Are we all giving up on studying for the history test?" I ask, arching an eyebrow at the stack of abandoned textbooks. "I mean, I'm not against it, I just wanted to confirm."

Lucas shrugs. "I think if I don't know it at this point, it's safe to say I'm not going to know it by tomorrow morning."

"If that's true, I'm screwed," Mike groans.

"I just can't stare at a textbook anymore," says Lucas. "My brain is going to melt if I try to read one more primary source."

"Okay," I say. "But for the record, if we all fail this test tomorrow, that is not on me."

"We're not gonna fail," says Lucas.

"Speak for yourself," says Mike. He doesn't seem too bothered, though, flipping through an old X-Men comic scooped up from some pile or another in the basement.

"Come on, dude, do your presentation and I'll quiz you," Lucas insists, shifting in his seat to give me his full attention, tucking one of the textbooks into his lap like it's a clipboard and he's ready to judge.

"Okay," I say. "Just go easy on me."

"No way," says Lucas. "Hard-hitting questions only."

I roll my eyes, but I can't help but laugh a little. It's nice, feeling like my friends actually care about this thing I'm doing, seeing them try to show interest and help out in their own small ways. I clear my throat and prepare to run through my presentation.

We spend a good hour with Lucas asking questions,

from the reasonable and technical to the absurd and everything in between. After a while, I feel confident I can answer anything the judges might throw at me. Hell, with my friends by my side, I think I can handle anything the world throws at me.

▶

When I get home from Mike's, my mom is in the living room watching *60 Minutes,* and she perks up to tell me that there's a letter from Will on the kitchen counter.

I drop my backpack and grab a glass of water, leaning against the island as I tear open the envelope. But it's not a full letter, just a short note accompanying a piece of thick vellum paper with artwork on it.

The note says:

Nov. 30, 1985

Dear Dustin,

Good luck at the science fair! If it's not too last minute to add to your poster, this is just something I was working on. No pressure, it's your project, after all. But maybe it could add some color and fun to the board!

Either way, I hope you have the best time

at the fair and I expect you to tell me everything once it's over.

Best,

Will


Then there's the art: an amazing, beautiful title card for my poster. The words THE BARD BOX are sketched in neat block letters, with intricate flourishes on either side that look like sound waves in a rainbow of colors. It's so awesome I could cry. My heart squeezes with gratitude that Will can still be part of the project, even all the way from California.

I can't wait to add it to my poster. I can't wait for the science fair! And I can't wait to share it all with my friends.

# CHAPTER FIFTEEN

## WEDNESDAY, DECEMBER 4, 1985

Overall, things feel really good leading into the weekend of the science fair. Between Will's art, Mike's proofreading, and Lucas's thorough interview prep, it almost feels like they are doing the project with me. Best of all, Lucas and Mike will be at the fair to cheer me on.

I feel on top of the world, like nothing could bring me down. Not even—

"I got on the basketball team!"

Mike and I are at the Hellfire Club table at lunch when Lucas darts up to us, practically vibrating with excitement. We turn to face him as the rest of Hellfire continue the conversation about where we left off in Eddie's campaign.

"Congrats, man," I say politely. Even though we've made up enough to be on speaking terms, the enthusiasm he surely expects is not something I can quite manage. I try for a smile, but I'm sure it looks like a wince. "I know you really wanted that."

I don't say, *For some ungodly reason.*

"Yeah, I guess you're officially, like, one of the jocks," Mike says, with even less enthusiasm than I'd mustered.

Lucas's excitement visibly wavers at our lackluster response.

"Yeah, I guess so," he says, shoving his hands in his pockets. His mouth twists into a sideways frown as he looks at me. "Look, anyway, the first practice of the season is this Saturday, so—"

"Are you kidding me?" I say. *Please, please be kidding me.*

Lucas shifts his weight and looks around the cafeteria, as if someone might swoop in and save him from this conversation. "I'm really sorry, dude, but I don't think I can come to the science fair."

"Can't you skip out on practice this once?" I ask.

"It's a big conditioning and orientation day," Lucas says, brows drawn together, like he really *does* regret it, but that doesn't change his words. "I'm sorry, Dustin, but you know this is important to me—"

"*This* is important to me, too!" I exclaim.

The Hellfire Club quiets at my raised voice, taking note of the brewing conflict.

"Wait, what's going on?" whispers Gareth as he leans in behind me.

"Leave it, dude," Eddie hisses.

"Look, maybe you can just leave your practice a little early?" Mike says to Lucas. "Nancy's driving me to Indianapolis in the afternoon, after her newspaper thing, just for the viewing and awards and all that."

Lucas grimaces. "I really don't want to make a bad impression on the coach, or the team—"

"And what about your *best friends,* Lucas?" I demand. "You don't have a problem making a bad impression on *them?*"

Lucas huffs out an exasperated sigh, shaking his head and throwing up his hands.

"I can . . . I can talk to the coach about leaving a *little bit* early," he says.

I perk right up. "Are you serious?" I ask. "Are you sure?"

"I'll *try,*" says Lucas. "I told you I'd go, and I know it's important to you. Just—you owe me to show up to at least *one* of my games, *without* complaining."

"Deal," I say. And because I'm aware it's a decently big sacrifice considering Lucas's priorities this year, I add, "Thank you. Seriously."

"Yeah," Lucas says, smiling, but it doesn't reach his eyes.

I'm relieved, but Lucas spends the rest of lunch quiet.

▶

I'm enthusing to Suzie about the science fair, and about making up with my friends, and Lucas getting on the basketball team, when she drops the bomb:

*"That doesn't sound like making up, Dusty-bun, it sounds like you guys didn't talk about the problem at all."*

"What are you talking about? We totally bonded over our fears and stuff. We're, like, all good now. I even told Lucas congratulations about getting on the basketball team, even though I still don't get it."

*"Exactly,"* Suzie says. *"You still don't get it. Have you actually talked about why he cares about basketball all of a sudden? Or have you told him why you're so afraid of losing him?"*

"That's not—" I huff. "You just don't get it. This is what we do, we fight, and we make up, but we're always friends." Even if we don't talk about problems unless they involve interdimensional monsters or evil Russians. "Besides, they're coming to the science fair, so it's going to be even more epic and amazing than it was already going to be."

*"Okay, Dusty,"* Suzie sighs. *"But, if you get the chance, promise me you guys will talk out your actual feelings?"*

*Ugh.* I adore Suzie, but between her and Robin, I've had enough *feelings* talk for the next year. But Suzie is a genius and the light of my life for a reason: she tends to be right.

"Okay, I hear you," I agree. But hopefully, everything is fine, and there won't be any need for that. "But anyway, what are you up to? Did you get your new computer set up?"

"I did!" she enthuses. She's been taking computer science classes at a local college, and her dad finally bought a personal computer for home use. It's crazy to think that that kind of technology will soon be in everyone's home. *"But I was actually just reading the next chapter of Neuromancer. If you haven't read it yet, I could read it aloud?"*

And I *have* read it, of course, because I prioritize our little book club over my homework most of the time. But I love Suzie's voice, and I'll take any excuse to listen to it, to hang out with her over the radio waves, like there isn't so much distance between us.

"That sounds perfect," I say.

The line goes quiet for a minute, presumably while Suzie is grabbing the book and flipping to where she left off.

She begins to read, and I let her voice transport me to new worlds.

# PART THREE

# CHAPTER SIXTEEN

## SATURDAY, DECEMBER 7, 1985

### *8:33 A.M.*

The day of the science fair dawns on my house, empty save for myself and Tews the cat. My mom spent all of last night showering me with hugs and kisses, fluttering around me, worrying about whether I'd really be okay without her. She acted like she was preparing to go to war for years, not just to Florida for a quick weekend. Despite my insistence that I would somehow find a way to survive without her, she still left a note on the counter with thorough instructions and a reminder of Aunt Kathy's number if I need to get in touch. Of course, she ends with many well wishes for the science fair. I feed Tews, eat some cereal, and prepare for the day.

In no time, I find myself waiting by the door with the Bard Box and my poster at my side, bouncing on my heels, perking up every time a car goes by. Finally, a van comes squealing to a stop in front of my house. It looks shabby and scrapped together in a way that might not be entirely safe, but I'm not a car guy, so who am I to judge? Music—which I can now recognize as Metallica—is blasting from the van as I burst out the door and hobble over, weighed down by my project.

Eddie hops out of the van and rushes over to take the poster from my hands.

"Well, Henderson, today's the day," he greets me, and opens the van's back doors to load everything in.

"Today's the day," I agree, equal parts excitement and trepidation coloring my voice.

I haul over the Bard Box, and we carefully arrange it in the back. The van's a bit messy: a few other pieces of musical equipment and some assorted junk, including a pair of boxers that I do *not* want to get close enough to investigate, clutter the back.

I'm nervous—not just about the fair, although that's certainly part of it, but about everything the day might bring. I'm already feeling the absence of my friends, but I'm trying to keep their treachery out of my head. Which just leaves me with Eddie, who I still can't believe agreed to help in the first place. I'm grateful, but I can't help but feel like I'm asking a lot of him, and I'm determined to be the best possible road trip buddy.

Eddie stands in front of the passenger-side door, blocking me from entering. He lifts up his chin so he can look down his nose at me, scrutinizing.

"A grand adventure awaits," he says in his DM's voice, which instantly has me standing at attention. "A treacherous road lies ahead of us. There may be obstacles. There *may* even be *monsters*. Are you sure you're ready to embark on this journey?"

I can't help but break into a grin.

"With great risk comes great reward," I say. "I'm ready to venture forth."

"Well then," Eddie says, biting back his own smile as he makes a sweeping gesture toward the passenger seat. "Your chariot awaits."

He moves out of the way and goes back to the driver's side, and I hop into the passenger seat, and then the van is lurching onto the road at a speed that seems questionable, but I politely do not say so.

And we're off.

Anticipation buzzes through me, and Eddie turns the volume up on a song I don't know, and the electric pulse of the guitars only energizes me more. After a minute, we're on the highway, with open road stretching ahead of us, the early-morning sun starting its ascent into the sky.

I dig through my backpack full of snacks to find my

trusty compass and map, where I've got the route and directions all planned out.

Eddie lets out a low, impressed whistle as I unfold the map.

"Dude, you're quite the navigator," he says.

"Just doing my duty as copilot," I say. "And I promised snacks, so I've got a full haul. If you want chips or candy or soda, I've got just about everything in here."

I don't say that I blew almost all the money my mom gave me for food for the weekend on a wide variety of snacks. I wasn't sure what Eddie would want, so I may have gone overboard getting a little bit of everything.

"Sounds good, man," Eddie says. "And, I told you I'd cover the music—you're listening right now to a custom road-trip mixtape made by yours truly. Some stuff you'll know, some stuff to continue your rock education."

As if on cue, the song shifts from one I didn't recognize to one I definitely do, with an iconic opening guitar riff. I smile as I look out the window, watching Hawkins disappear behind us and endless fields of corn appear before us. The drums come in, and I remember Eddie's advice—*if you're not headbanging, it doesn't count*—and start bobbing my head to the beat.

Eddie casts me a grin and starts nodding his head too.

The raspy vocals come in and Eddie sings along, turning the music up even louder, until each drumbeat rattles the car and vibrates in my bones. Laughter bubbles up in my chest, light and free. I decide to try my hand at air drums, banging at the air with my hands in an attempt at matching the rhythm. As the music builds to the chorus, Eddie drums his palms against the steering wheel. I chime in for the chorus, because I actually know the lyrics to that bit.

We totally jam out, shouting the lyrics as we race down the highway. Eddie even manages a decent air guitar solo before I punch him in the arm.

"Hands on the wheel, Munson!" I have to shout over the music. "There's nothing metal about vehicular manslaughter."

"Are you kidding me?" Eddie shouts back. "Vehicular Manslaughter sounds like a totally killer name for a metal band."

"Pun intended?" I ask.

"What?"

"Totally killer?" I say. "*Killer?* No?"

Eddie looks at me for a long moment, shaking his head as if disappointed, but then his expression melts into the wavering of a held-back smile. After a beat, he throws his head back laughing.

I let out a giggle, and by then the chorus is rolling back around, so we get back to singing at the top of our lungs.

▶

I'm hanging half out the window as Eddie pumps gas into the van, head slumped on my folded arms. We'd passed a good half hour rocking out to music, and then I'd introduced a game of "Would You Rather" to pass the time.

"Would you rather," I start, "fight one owlbear-size duck or a hundred duck-size owlbears?"

Eddie, slotting the gas nozzle into place, doesn't hesitate. "Oh, duck-size owlbears, hands down."

My head pops up from the pillow of my arms. "No way," I say, scandalized. "Why?"

Eddie raises his brows and scoffs as he reaches through the window to grab his abandoned bag of chips from the driver's seat. "Have you ever looked a duck in the eye?"

"Can't say that I have," I say.

"Well, they're evil. Pure evil," he says, absently munching on the chips as the gas pumps. "Owlbears, at least, are neutrally aligned—"

"No, okay, no! You're just wrong!" I burst out. "You are so unbelievably wrong, it's not even funny."

"That's my opinion!" His mouth is full, so the words come out muffled and he sprays potato chip crumbs in my direction. "You asked me a question, that's my answer."

I practically lurch out the window in the offense I take to his decision.

"You think you can take a *hundred* owlbears, Eddie?" I demand. "A *hundred*?"

"They're duck-size! It'd be like Whac-A-Mole, I'd just swat them away." He illustrates this with a gesture like he's swinging a baseball bat.

"Owlbears have an armor class on par with chain mail, dude," I point out.

"And ducks," Eddie says, "have eyes that can look into your soul and do *irreparable* psychic damage."

The gas pump clicks, telling us the tank is full and ready to go. Eddie gives me a withering look, pivots to put the nozzle back on its hook and throws the empty bag of chips in the trash.

Amusement crowds the edges of my outrage as I realize Eddie is serious. I hold it in for a long minute as he crosses back to the driver's side, swings himself inside, slams the door shut, turns the key in the ignition. Finally, I ask, delighted—

"Is this duck thing something we should unpack?"

"Don't worry about it," says Eddie. "Worry about yourself, and the owlbear-size duck you have to fight."

▶

In an hour of driving, I've learned that Eddie likes to drive *fast,* so when he suddenly slows down to the highway speed limit, I'm almost concerned.

"Everything okay?" I ask.

"Yep," he says, lifting one hand from the wheel to point ahead at a bridge crossing over the highway. "This bridge tends to be a speed trap."

I'm not sure what he means until we pass under the

bridge, and sure enough, a police car is parked just out of view on the side of the road. Eddie gives the cruiser a wave, wiggling his fingers.

As soon as the bridge and police car are no longer in the rearview mirror, Eddie steps on the gas and brings us back to a reckless pace.

"How'd you know that?" I ask.

"Oh, you drive the highways enough times, you figure out all their little tricks," he says. "I'll credit that one to good ole Dad, though. One of the only useful things he ever taught me."

I huff a laugh. "The only life lessons I learned from my dad were how *not* to act."

"I'll drink to that," Eddie says, taking a swig from his can of Coke. Then, "You don't mention your dad that much."

I shrug one shoulder. My dad's not something I talk about much or even dwell on.

"He lives in Illinois now," I say. "We don't really keep in touch."

"Ah, a fellow member of the deadbeat dad club?" Eddie asks with a sympathetic wince.

"I mean, kind of? He was more just . . . an asshole?" I say. "He cheated on my mom when I was a kid, they divorced, she moved us back to Hawkins where they'd both grown up, and that's kind of it."

I was too much of a mama's boy at that age to forgive

my dad, and he didn't care enough to work past that, and now our relationship is nonexistent.

Eddie lets out a low whistle that seems to say *sheesh*. "Sounds like a dick," he says.

"Eh," I say. "I'm not really bothered."

As far as I'm concerned, my dad has nothing to do with me. If anything, the way he treated my mom makes me more determined to treat my mom better, and Suzie too. I don't want to be anything like him.

Everything that makes me *me,* I owe to my mom, and my friends, and *myself.* Walter Henderson gets no claim in how awesome I am, thank you very much.

"Good on you, dude," says Eddie. "Hey"—he scoops up his can of Coke and extends it to me in cheers—"screw 'em, right?"

"Yeah," I laugh, tapping my own soda against his. "Screw 'em."

▶

It might be the excessive amount of Bugles I've eaten in the past half hour, but by the time we're approaching the Indianapolis convention center, I can see the first hints of the science fair around us—a few people headed the same direction hauling projects and poster boards with family and friends in tow—and I'm abuzz with nervous excitement. Best-case and worst-case scenarios flutter through my head in equal measure. What if they hate the project so much I'm banned from ever returning? What if they love it, and I win, and for good measure, I'm promised a career at a top tech company after graduation? What if I turn the Bard Box on in front of the judges and it spontaneously combusts? What if—

"Man, you're really showing that can who's boss," Eddie says, his voice pulling me from my own head.

I blink rapidly to refocus, tearing my gaze from the streets of Indianapolis. And I realize that I've been taking my nerves out on my empty soda can, which is now crumpled and misshapen in my hand.

"I think I had too much junk food," I say.

We're coming up on the new convention center now, all sleek glass and steel and brick, with endless windows. It's an impressive building, massive, and so different from anything we have in small-town Hawkins. The entrance is bustling with people, and I swallow hard. I feel like I'm staring down the entrance to a dungeon that I *know* is going to wipe out the party's resources.

"You know, it's okay to be nervous," Eddie says.

"I'm not nervous," I lie.

"Sure," he says, clearly not buying it but being kind. "But if you *were,* that'd be okay."

I disagree. It feels so juvenile to be nervous about a science fair. I bet Eddie doesn't get nervous about *anything.*

"I know." My voice goes the kind of high-pitched it only does when I'm lying.

Eddie turns the van into the conference center parking garage and makes his way through a sea of cars, looking for an open space.

"Let me tell you a secret," Eddie says. "I still get nervous before *every* gig with Corroded Coffin."

"No way," I protest.

"Cross my heart," he says, hand over his chest. "No matter how many times I do it, or how many times we've practiced the songs on the set list, there's always a moment before we start where I'll be standing there with my guitar like, *am I actually going to do this?*"

It's weird to think of Eddie like that, when he usually seems so bold and fearless. But I guess everyone's scared of something.

"And . . . how do you get yourself to do it?" I ask.

"Honestly, I don't have a frigging clue," Eddie snorts. "I'm not brave, man, I'm not facing my fears. I just . . . love music, more than I'm afraid of everything else."

And I think I get that. I think science might be like that, for me.

"And then suddenly I'm playing, and my friends are up there with me, and everything's fine," he finishes.

I look at Eddie, who's turning the steering wheel hand over hand as we pull into a parking space, and am hit with gratitude that he's here with me so I'm not going in there totally alone. Maybe my friends aren't coming until later, but Eddie's here now, and that counts for something.

It counts for a lot, actually.

Eddie puts the car in park and turns to me.

"So?" he asks.

I nod, small at first, then more certain.

I won't abandon this quest. I set out on a mission, and I will finish it.

"Okay," I say, steeling myself. "Okay. Let's do this."

# CHAPTER SEVENTEEN

## SATURDAY, DECEMBER 7, 1985
## 10:04 A.M.

The convention center is even more overwhelming once we find our way inside. Banners welcome everyone to the Science and Engineering Fair of Indiana, the walls are adorned with signs for the event with fun science facts, and registration tables line the back wall. And at the center of all of that is a sea of people with projects of all kinds. People carry everything from baking soda volcanoes to homemade wind turbines and trebuchets to bulky contraptions I couldn't possibly identify from afar. And of course, everyone has a poster board.

Everywhere I look is science. I'm positively *surrounded* by nerds. It's enough to make me giddy.

Eddie falls into step behind me, letting me lead the way. He's got my poster under his arm, and I'm lugging the Bard Box along with care. He's taking everything in too, and I can't help but notice how out of place he looks among so many cliché nerdy types. I'd bet he's the only person in the building wearing a stitch of leather.

As I head toward the registration table for last names F through J, the crowd around us shifts to give us room, and I notice more than one person giving Eddie a skeptical look. I get that he's a scary-looking guy, but it's a bit over the top how people spread out like we're contagious.

"Tough crowd," Eddie mutters.

"Not a lot of overlap between the science nerds and the metalheads, I guess," I say.

"You and Wheeler weren't that much better when we first met," Eddie reminds me.

Which is fair enough, but I can only hope people here might see Eddie as more than the scary-looking guy he seems to be at first glance.

I come to a stop at the registration table.

"Last name, Henderson," I tell the woman. "Dustin Henderson."

She shuffles through a filing box of folders, finger running down through the H's before she finds me.

"Ah, here we are," she says, pulling out a folder and

handing it to me. "And is this, uh, Mr. Henderson Senior?" She eyes Eddie warily.

Eddie offers a cheery wave.

"Nope," I say, offering a smile and no further details.

"Right," she says, uncertain, tearing her attention away from Eddie and back to the folder. "Well, this has the schedule for the day, your name tag and your assigned display booth in the expo hall, and which group you're in for judging sessions. You'll want to get your booth set up, but there's plenty of time to do that, chat with your fellow scientists, and check out the displays from all our sponsors and special guests. Okay?"

"Sounds good," I say, tucking the folder under my arm, my hands full with the Bard Box. "Thanks."

I turn to figure out the way to the expo hall, eager to get everything set up before I explore. I spot the sign pointing to where we need to go, but I don't get far before Eddie catches my arm.

"Hey, I gotta take a leak," he says. "I'll find you at your booth, okay?"

I have a strange, childlike urge to say, *Don't leave meee,* but this is a solo quest, and sometimes, even your closest allies can't help with that. So I leave Eddie to find my spot, Bard Box and poster in tow.

When I arrive at the expo hall, I find what seems like endless rows and rows of tables, countless students settling into their spots and putting their presentations in place with help from friends and family. As I look for my spot, I sneak a peek at the projects I pass. Some of the posters are really imaginative and illustrated, others more plain and straightforward. Some projects have displays or devices or live components, some just have photos and their presentation. They represent a broad range of sciences, from engineering (like mine) to biochemistry and environmental science, and everything in between. Some are completely cobbled together in fascinating ways, like a motorized Barbie car with knives taped to either side that is advertised as a "self-driving lawn mower." Except, it's in a cage and keeps bumping up against the boundaries with a *clangclangclang* like someone forgot to include a stopping mechanism.

God, science is cool.

I find the spot I've been assigned, and I set down the Bard Box and exhale, taking it all in. Just being here, surrounded by so much excitement and curiosity and passion—it's invigorating. And sure, we did the local science fair all through middle school as a party, but this is at a different scale, a whole new level. Mike and Lucas are going to *freak* when they see this.

I see a girl approaching a neighboring booth with two big plants in her arms, teetering and on the verge of falling down, and I rush over, eager for the distraction. I catch the bigger, leafier of the two plants just as it's about to topple over.

"Careful there," I say, hoisting it up by its pot.

Without the tree in her face, I can see she has long, dark

hair and brown skin, and she blinks at me wide-eyed. With one hand freed, she pushes up the thick-framed glasses sliding down her nose.

"Thanks," she says. Her voice is quiet and gentle but tinged with suspicion, like she doesn't comprehend why I would help her.

She shuffles over to the booth next to mine and puts down the plant, and I follow suit. She arranges the plants on the table, but there's no poster explaining what her project is.

I survey the plants, one of which is an average, leafy green tomato plant. The other is massively oversize, and somehow even more vibrantly green, its leaves grand and shining. On each plant, there are a few red tomatoes, but on the superplant, the tomatoes are bigger than fists.

I don't know a lot about gardening, but I know that whatever's been done to that plant, it's a damn-near miracle.

"This is amazing," I say, genuine awe coloring my voice.

"Thanks," the girl says again, and continues to regard me warily while avoiding direct eye contact.

"I'm Dustin," I say, offering a toothy smile. I point at my own setup. "Looks like we're neighbors."

"I'm Anika," she says. She doesn't offer a handshake, or even a smile. I don't let it deter me.

"What's your project, anyway? That's, like, the Hulk of tomato plants," I say.

Anika glances at the plants, then back at me.

"I investigated the effects of various solutions on plant

growth in the hopes of creating a sustainable path to global food security," she says, which I can only guess is her rehearsed pitch or else she simply talks like that. I don't know which option weirds me out more. She points to the plants. "I monitored these plants over sixty days of growth. The smaller one grew naturally. The bigger one used a small amount of my growth solution every day. I believe this solution could be used to end world hunger by the year 2000."

"Oh, wow," I say. I jerk a thumb over my shoulder toward my booth. "I made a box? That makes music? It's called Bard Box. Like . . . like Dungeons and Dragons?"

Somehow, that seems less impressive next to Anika's plant that's going to solve world hunger.

"Right," Anika says. "I have to go grab my poster."

She abruptly turns and walks off.

I watch her for a moment, unsure if it was something I said, or if she's just . . . like that.

"Whoa," someone says behind me. I nearly jump out of my skin and whirl around to see who it is. "Did you just *talk* to *Anika*?"

"Damn, you scared me," I say as I find my booth neighbor on the opposite side has returned to his display, which appears to be some sort of water filtration system. "But, uh, yeah? I guess so."

The boy has pale skin and neatly trimmed dark hair. He's also in formal dress, jacket and tie and everything. I can't help but feel a bit underdressed next to him. All I did was wear a *slightly* nicer button-up shirt than usual over a graphic tee that spells out genius using elements of the periodic table: germanium, nickel, uranium, and sulfur.

"Bold," the guy says, about my outfit or Anika or both. "Everyone knows you don't talk to Anika on fair days, if at all."

I laugh at first, assuming he's joking, but his intense stare doesn't waver.

"Oh, like actually?" I say. "Why?"

"She says she needs to get in the right headspace," says the boy, raising his brows like that's ridiculous. "But it's not like she needs it, she's gone to ISEF the last two years."

He's lost me there. What the hell is eye-seph?

"Eye-seph?" I ask.

"The International Science and Engineering Fair?" Like it should be obvious.

"Oh," I say. I'm feeling a bit out of my depth with this kid, and that's not a feeling I like.

"Are you new to this?" I don't think he means it to be patronizing, but that's how it comes out.

"To this particular fair, yeah," I say. "I've done local ones at my school, but this is . . . a little different."

"I'll bet," he says. "I'm Brian."

He shoves out his hand for a handshake. I take it, and he practically rips my arm out of its socket with how vigorously he shakes it.

"Dustin," I say.

"You must not go to Eastwood, or I'd recognize you," Brian says. "I know most everyone."

"Uh, no, where's that? I'm from Hawkins, in Indiana."

"Wow, you really are a newbie," he laughs. "Eastwood Academy, in Ohio? It's only the most prestigious science- and technology-focused school in the region, if not the country. A lot of the people here go there. Anika, of course, and me and my project partner, and a bunch of people who went to ISEF last year. This stuff is our lifeblood."

"That sounds intense," I say. "My school's mostly preoccupied with sports and who's screwing who under which bleachers."

"I'll bet," Brian says again, a bit smug. "It's nice to be somewhere where being smart makes you cool."

"I can imagine," I say.

But it's hard to imagine, actually—a whole *school* of science nerds who take this stuff seriously? It must be a utopia compared to the primitive Hawkins High. No jocks versus nerds, no inane social hierarchies, just people who care about knowledge and curiosity and wonder. I'm almost salivating at the thought. What if being smart made you *cool,* instead of a target?

"Anyway, I have to get everything set up for my project, but I'll see you around," Brian says.

Before I can say anything else, he turns back to his project, effectively dismissing me.

Anika returns to her station with her poster, and I feel a bit sheepish with both my neighbors paying me no mind as they work diligently on their world-saving projects. They're awesome, but it makes me wonder if the Bard Box is missing some hidden criteria for the fair. It's not like I don't want to make the world a better place, but can't that be done through cool stuff? Through fun?

"Damn, Henderson." Eddie's voice comes from behind me, and it fills me with relief. "I don't know why I was picturing a dinky little nerd-fest, but this is, like, the real deal."

"You're telling me," I say.

I'm ridiculously proud of the Bard Box, but I'm a little intimidated by the level of quality in the projects I've seen so far. I want so badly to do well, to impress my friends, to give them something awesome to support when they're coming all this way.

But I'm starting to think I don't have a shot, and my friends are going to come here just to be disappointed. I can already imagine Mike's strained expression and him saying something about how winning isn't everything, like that's some sort of consolation. Maybe they'll think it was a waste of a long drive each way. Maybe Lucas will regret prioritizing me and my fair over his basketball practice.

I'm pulled out of my spiral when something shatters across the hall. There's a collective gasp as everyone swivels toward the sound. Then—

An agonized scream.

*"My telescope!"*

It's shrill, anguished. And followed immediately by sobbing.

I can't see anything past the sea of poster boards, but

everyone in the hall is looking toward the sound with concern and pity. God, what a tough break. If something happened to the Bard Box this late in the game, I'd be devastated.

"Looks like the curse is starting early this year," Brian mutters.

I turn around and look at Brian, who's smoothing down the edges of the papers glued on his poster.

"Sorry, curse?" I ask.

"Right, you wouldn't know," he says, ditching his poster to face me fully. "It's kind of a legend at this fair in particular. Every year, perfectly good projects start going haywire at the last minute."

"God, that's bad luck," I say with a sympathetic wince.

"It's not just luck," Brian says darkly. "It's *real*."

"Come on, seriously?" I ask. He seems so intensely into science that I find it hard to believe he buys into something as superstitious as a curse.

"Seriously," says Brian. "Look, do you see that boy?" He points to a kid who is shuffling through note cards, talking to himself, rehearsing his presentation. "That's David Liu. Last year, he had this super-elaborate terrarium ecosystem, but the morning of, it flooded and was moldy by judging."

"Okay, but that doesn't mean anything," I say. "Maybe it was easier to blame his mistake on a curse than to admit he messed up—"

"Yeah, but the year before that," Brian interrupts, "Heather MacArthur was a shoo-in to win with this solar panel made from recycled materials. That is, until it caught fire out of nowhere, right in front of the judges, in the middle of her presentation."

"Crap," I say.

"She hasn't shown her face at a fair since," Brian says, shaking his head like it's a great shame.

"I mean, it sounds improbable, sure," I say, "but couldn't it have been an accident?"

"Maybe," he says, "but the year before *that*, my very first time here, it happened to me. My water filtration system got clogged and backed up, and an essential pipe burst and sprayed a judge right in the eye. I might never live that down."

My mind is moving a mile a minute. Once is a mistake, twice is a coincidence, but three project failures is a *pattern*. I don't know that I believe there's a *curse*. I mean, the whole *alternate dimensions leaking into our world* thing makes me open to believe there's a lot more going on in our lives than we can explain, but that particular can of worms has always been specific to Hawkins. Curse or not, though, *something's* going on here. I'd be lying if I said the possibility of it doesn't thrill me a little—there's a real, bona fide mystery going on here, and I think myself uniquely qualified to uncover it.

"This year is my last chance at redemption before I graduate," Brian says. "My filtration system is better than ever, and I'm not letting a curse or anything stand in my way."

I don't point out that theoretical curses probably don't care about intentions or redemption, because I'm too busy thinking about the mystery at hand.

"Right," I say absently. "Good luck with that."

Brian offers an unenthused smile before turning back to his project, and I turn back to Eddie, who's been watching the interaction with a disapproving expression.

"Is it just me, or was that kid kind of a tool?" Eddie whispers.

I wave him off immediately, brain moving too rapidly and excitedly to bother responding. "More importantly, did you hear that? There's a *curse,* Eddie!" Perhaps a bit too gleefully.

"Yeah, I heard," Eddie says. "Why do you seem so happy about that?"

"Don't you see? *This* is my quest!" I say. "This is why I'm here! I might not be able to win the science fair, but I can get to the bottom of this and save the day!"

"Ah, I see," Eddie says. "Your valiant quest has a new goal: break the curse."

God, imagine how excited Mike and Lucas would be if they got here and I could tell them I solved a great mystery, all by myself. I can almost picture it now—how they'd enthuse, and ask questions, and demand the full, unabridged tale of my adventure. Max would be there too, and even Will and El, all the way from California, and they'd chant my name and lift me on their shoulders and then we'd all go play D&D like we used to, and—

Speakers crackle to life from every corner of the massive

expo hall, and a pleasant voice informs us—

*"Everyone, please make your way to Ballroom C for the opening address, which will start in five minutes. There will be more time to set up before judging begins."*

I scan the hall as people slowly start migrating toward the exit, including Anika, though Brian fiddles with his poster a moment longer.

"Shall we?" Eddie asks, nodding toward the doors. But just as I'm about to nod and lead us out, I hear shouting to my left.

"Frodo! Frodo, get back here!"

At the same time, Eddie lets out what can only be described as a squeak and says, "Oh, what the— Goddammit!" as he almost knocks over my table in his desperation to get away from—

A duck, which waddles toward him completely innocuously.

I blink down at the duck. It blinks up at me. Lets out a little quack. I put the Bard Box down and scoop the duck up in my hands as gently as I can.

"For Christ's sake, don't touch it," Eddie hisses.

A boy pushes through the crowd and comes skidding to a stop in front of me, panting.

"Frodo!" he gasps, taking the duck out of my hands and cradling him against his chest. "Oh, thank goodness."

He's got light hair and freckles and a round face, and he strokes the duck lovingly. When I glance over, Eddie is keeping us at a yard's distance and watching the duck with great suspicion.

"Is that duck named Frodo?" I ask. "Like, Frodo Baggins?"

"Frodo Quackins," the boy corrects me. He's got a thick Southern accent, which makes his answer impossibly funnier.

"Whoa, that's amazing," I say. I crouch to coo at the duck, "You're pretty far from the Shire, aren't you?" Then, to the boy, "Uh, forgive Eddie, he has a thing about ducks, apparently."

The boy casts glances toward Eddie, amused, not intimidated in the slightest. But I suppose no amount of leather and long hair can outweigh seeing a grown man cowering at the sight of a duck.

"No offense taken, Frodo's a biter, so being scared is the appropriate response," the boy says, smoothing a ruffled section of feathers, and Frodo nips at his fingers as if to prove his point. "Thank you for catching him, though, seriously. He would have led me on a wild goose chase around the whole dang building if not for you."

"Duck chase," I can't help but say.

"What?" he asks.

"Wild . . . duck chase?" I wince, but the boy throws back his head and laughs.

"You're so right, my gosh," he says. "I'm Danny, by the way. Are you a first-timer too?"

"Dustin," I say. "And yeah . . . am I obvious or something?"

"No, you just seem less intense than some of the really competitive guys," Danny says with a little shrug. "Look,

162

I've gotta give Mr. Quackins some fresh air, or else he'll rebel and try to give me the slip again. You're welcome to join me if you don't mind skipping the opening address. Frodo can show you his tricks, and you can show me what that mystery machine does." He nods to the Bard Box behind me and I grin.

I look to Eddie, who shrugs like, *your choice.* I don't necessarily want to skip the opening, though it's mostly housekeeping stuff, but I can't say I'm not beyond fascinated by the idea of this duck doing tricks. I almost wonder if the *duck* could be ruining projects. At the very least, maybe Danny knows something about this curse, and it'd be good to get his perspective.

Besides, he's kind of the first person I've met so far who doesn't feel like they're judging me and the Bard Box. He's the first person who's asked about my project at all.

"Uh, sure," I say. "Lead the way, Frodo Quackins."

"Great!" Danny says. "I'll go grab his leash, give me just a sec!"

Danny runs off with Frodo in his arms while I'm still processing the fact that there are *leashes* for *ducks.* Eddie finally returns to my side with a sheepish look.

"I'll let you handle this one alone," he says. "I'm all for you making friends, but does it have to be . . ."

I raise my eyebrows, unable to hide my amusement. Everyone thinks Eddie's so tough, but here he is, rendered useless by a common waterfowl.

"Dude, I can't believe you're *actually* afraid of ducks," I say.

He glares at me. "Speak a word of this to *anyone,* Henderson, I swear to God—"

"Your secret's safe with me," I vow.

Mostly because no one would ever believe me.

▶

Danny and I leave Eddie to follow the crowds out of the expo hall. I have the Bard Box in tow. Frodo is now hooked up to an unfairly adorable blue leash and harness, waddling along ahead of us, better leash-trained than some dogs I've seen.

Danny navigates the long hallways of the convention center with ease, bringing us out of the central rush of fair festivities and into a quieter area of the convention center.

"So, I have to ask . . . ," I say. "Why the duck?"

Danny laughs. "Why not?" he asks. "It's fun, isn't it?"

"Yeah, definitely," I say. "But it's a far cry from everyone else in there trying to solve the energy crisis, or whatever."

Danny waves his hand, like the energy crisis is petty drama he doesn't care for. "Science is supposed to be fun, if you ask me. I think a lot of the people here forget that."

I nod, thinking about Anika's quiet intensity, Brian's holier-than-thou attitude conveyed through passive-aggressive remarks.

"Yeah, I get that," I say.

We reach the end of a hallway where there are doors leading outside to a loading dock. Danny opens the door and gestures me through before following with Frodo. The area is secluded, leaving us in a quiet area between buildings.

"But to answer your question seriously," Danny says as he reaches into his pocket for a plastic packet. He pours a mixture of seeds and corn into his hand, then scatters it on the ground, and Frodo eagerly starts pecking at it. "I help out on my family's farm with all the animals, back in Kentucky, and I just adore them, obviously. But I also love science, you know, and how it can intersect with agriculture to make things better on the farm, both for animals and people." He lights up with passion as he talks about it, smiling down at Frodo like a proud parent. "As for Frodo, he's just about the most intelligent creature I've ever met, and I thought it'd be neat to show that off."

"I've never thought of ducks as particularly intelligent," I admit.

Danny squats next to Frodo and covers the sides of his head, where his ears must be. "Don't say such things where Frodo can hear you!" he gasps. "He's sensitive."

The duck does not seem bothered, shaking off Danny's hands to continue pecking at a piece of corn on the ground.

"Sorry, Frodo," I say, simultaneously chastised and amused. "I'm sure you're very capable."

Danny smiles, satisfied, and stands up. He holds out his hand over Frodo's head.

"Frodo, high five!" he says.

Frodo jumps up to tap his beak against Danny's hand,

wings fluttering slightly. I laugh, delighted.

Danny keeps his hand out, palm up.

"Come on up," he says, and Frodo's wings flutter hard as he jumps and lands in Danny's outstretched hand, looking content as anything. "Good duck."

Okay, the whole thing is ridiculous, but I'd be crazy not to be impressed.

"That's the coolest thing I've ever seen," I say. "I actually have a bit of animal-handling experience myself."

I'm thinking back to D'Artagnan, the demodog I fostered, and our bond, forged through the power of nougat, before El closed the gate and Dart presumably died.

I hope they have 3 Musketeers in monster heaven.

"Oh, amazing! What animals do you work with?" Danny asks, letting Frodo back down to continue snacking.

*Would you believe me if I said a creature from another dimension?* I don't say.

Raising a Demogorgon whose only trick was *not* killing me and my friends is a bit different from a duck who can give high fives. Of course, all of that is classified information, so I swallow it down, clearing my throat.

"Uh, just, you know. My mom's cats." I try not to visibly wince at my own idiocy, and rush to change the subject. "How did Frodo get away from you earlier, anyway? You don't think it has to do with the curse, do you?"

"Goodness, no," says Danny. "No, he let himself out. Mama told me I'd regret teaching him how to unlatch his crate. I don't believe in that curse business anyhow."

"Why not?" I ask.

"Oh, on my family's old farm? I've seen ghosts, and I've seen curses. This ain't that."

I'm trying to process how casually he talks about ghosts and curses, but then, with my own experiences with the supernatural, who am I to judge?

"Wait, so you *do* believe in curses?" I ask. "You just don't think *this* one's real?"

"Gosh, it's just—classic teen bullying, if you ask me," Danny says with a shrug. "Things get too competitive, people start sabotaging each other. Curses are ancient, they're natural. This is too solid. Man-made. You know what I mean?"

And, somehow, I kind of do.

"I just hope they stay away from Frodo," Danny continues. "And, uh, that newfangled device you've got over there, of course. What does it do anyhow?"

I begin to turn my attention to the Bard Box, ready to launch into the explanation and demonstration I have rehearsed, but something about the idea of a serial saboteur at large isn't sitting right with me. Because they can't sabotage the Bard Box when it's here with me. But then—

*Son of a bitch.*

"There's a whole room of projects left alone during the opening address," I realize. "If someone is sabotaging projects, this would be the perfect opportunity."

The idea sends a thrill through me, and I realize I'm *excited.* Maybe that's wrong, when there's someone at large wreaking havoc. But there's purpose in the chaos, and I've always thrived under pressure. If there's a mystery here to be solved, then goddamn it, I'm going to solve it.

Danny's eyes widen. "You don't think—"

"Grab Frodo," I say, already in motion. "We're going to catch them in the act."

"Wow," says Danny, scrambling after me. "This is a whole . . . *scheme!*" He's charmingly delighted by it. "The most excitement I get down on the farm is when the goats pick fights among themselves."

"You're certainly not in Kansas anymore," I say. "Or, uh, Kentucky."

Frodo quacks, as if in agreement.

I grab the Bard Box, and Danny grabs Frodo, and we head back inside with new purpose.

This is no longer just a science fair; there's a saboteur among us.

And we're the only ones who can stop them.

▶

We burst through the doors of the expo hall only to find rows of projects and not a person in sight.

I don't know what I was expecting—someone in a full burglar getup in the middle of cutting wires or stealing vital components, maybe?

But there's nothing, and no one.

"Huh," says Danny. "Well, that was anticlimactic."

I frown as I venture farther down one of the rows,

looking around for anything out of place. But everything is quiet, and still, and normal.

"Yeah, I guess so," I say.

Just then, a click echoes across the hall as a set of doors opens. I act on pure instinct, grabbing Danny and immediately ducking behind a table. What if this is the saboteur? We can catch them in the act! I rush to press the button on the Bard Box that starts a new recording. Danny opens his mouth to say something, but I press my finger to my lips to tell him to keep quiet.

"What if someone finds it?" says a voice.

Even though they're across the large hall from us, the voice echoes through the room, clear as day.

"They're not gonna find it," says another voice. "Only a few people even *know* about the clubhouse."

I have no idea what they're talking about, but their hushed voices, and the fact that they're here instead of at the opening address, tells me it's nothing good. The second voice isn't totally unfamiliar, but I can't place it. I've heard so many new voices today.

"Why wouldn't you just destroy it?"

I'm gathering up the nerve to peek out from behind the table to see what's going on when—

Frodo lets out a loud quack.

There's a long stretch of silence. Then—

"Did you hear that?" someone whispers.

"I think it's just a bird that got inside or something," hisses the other person. "Come on, let's get back before people notice we're gone."

The sound of footsteps fades, and we hear the doors open and close again, and I finally let out a breath.

"Do you think that was . . . ," Danny starts.

"Whoever's sabotaging projects?" I finish. Then, "It sounds like it."

We emerge from under the table, Frodo waddling around blissfully ignorant. I stalk toward where the voices had lingered for a moment, looking for what they might have been doing. I'm not seeing anything until—

"Oh no," says Danny.

I follow Danny's line of sight, my breath catching when I think he's looking at *my* booth, even though I have the Bard Box with me. But it's not my booth. It's the booth next to mine.

Where a monstrously large tomato plant used to be, sits a sad, withered, shriveled, decidedly *dead* plant. It's not just the opposite of the plant I'd seen at Anika's booth earlier— it's an entirely different one, with a different pot, and not a tomato in sight.

"What do we do?" asks Danny. "Should we . . . tell someone?"

*What if someone finds it?* the voice asked. Which means—

"We need to find Anika," I say. "I think her plant is still out there." I pat the Bard Box. "And I think the people responsible are on this recording."

# CHAPTER
# EIGHTEEN

## SATURDAY, DECEMBER 7, 1985
## 11:16 A.M.

Danny and I find our way back to the main lobby around the same time the opening address ends. Everything is bustling again as people spread out in all directions, heading to their booths, or the sponsor section, or one of the workshops. With all the foot traffic, Danny scoops up Frodo. I scan the crowd, keeping an eye out for anything else amiss, as we search for Anika.

I spot Eddie near the entrance to the hall, leaning against a wall, looking menacing enough that the crowds are giving him a wide berth, like his personal bubble has an impenetrable four-foot radius. I wave at him and he perks up as we join him in lingering by the expo hall doors, watching people filter inside.

"Well, you missed out on a riveting speech from a long-winded school recruiter with a bow tie and a handlebar mustache," Eddie says, then regards Frodo warily with a wrinkled nose, keeping a safe distance. "I see the duck is still present."

I don't bother to even acknowledge this statement of the obvious.

"Hi," says Danny, sunny as ever, oblivious to or just not caring about Eddie's disdain.

"Act casual," I tell Eddie, glancing around to make sure everyone is wrapped up in their own conversations. "Everything is *fine.*"

"Everything *is* fine," Eddie laughs. "I mean, aside from the duck situation."

"We overheard these guys talking about sabotaging someone's project," I whisper. "We're keeping an eye out for any possible suspects."

"Sorry, what?" Eddie says, voice going loud and high-pitched. "Suspects? Sabotage?"

"I said *act casual,*" I hiss. "And yes, keep up."

Eddie rolls his eyes but schools his face into neutrality.

"Just break it down for the non-geniuses in the room?" he asks.

"We're doing an epic team-up to stop the bad guys before it's too late," Danny says, not bothering to veil his delight in the slightest. "Go team!"

"Wow," says Eddie. "You're . . . perky."

"Thank you," says Danny. Then earnestly tells him, "You know, my mama would kill for hair like yours."

Eddie gives a skeptical look, first to Danny, then to me, like, *are you going to do something about this?* When I say nothing, Eddie sighs and says, "Okay, kid," with an air of defeat.

I see Anika in the crowd, heading into the expo hall. I speed up to fall into step beside her, Danny and Eddie trailing.

"Anika!" I say. "Hey!"

As soon as she turns to eye me suspiciously, I realize I don't know how to do this.

"Um," I say. "Listen, I have good news and bad news. Do you, uh, have a preference? For the order of delivery?"

"What are you talking about?" she asks.

She's still walking with purpose through the expo hall, and I'm struggling to keep up my pace. Any moment now, she'll see her booth—and the dead plant.

Danny darts up and tries to block Anika's path.

"Why don't we all take a minute?" he suggests. "Pause, take a breather, have a little chat—"

"I'm sorry, I don't know what this is," Anika says, circumnavigating Danny's blockade and continuing to walk. "But I'm really just trying to get through the day. Do you guys mind—"

She cuts off, and I can pinpoint the exact moment she sees it, because she stops in her tracks for a heartbeat, jaw dropping.

Then she *sprints* over to her table, touching the dead

plant like she has to make sure it's real.

Danny and I rush over to her side, with Eddie following.

"This is impossible," Anika whispers, mournfully cupping the plant's dead leaves in her hands. "This can't be happening."

"I'm so sorry," Danny says softly.

"Maybe it just needs more water?" Eddie asks.

Danny, Anika, and I turn to glare at him in unison.

"Or less water?" he corrects, shrugging. "I'm not good with plants."

"Clearly," I say.

Anika drops the plant's drooping leaves and whirls on us with fire in her eyes.

"All right, this is really funny. Hilarious, even. Congrats, you got me! Now, where is it?"

"What?" I say. "This—this wasn't us!"

"Oh, what, it was the *curse,* then?" she asks. "Do you expect me to believe that?"

"This is no curse," I say. "This is foul play. But it wasn't us."

"We have proof!" Danny says. "And we're going to figure out who did it!"

I nod, attempting to be encouraging, but I'm less enthusiastic and less convinced than Danny is.

Anika grimaces as she looks between us in bewilderment, rage dissipating as tears well in her eyes. "I don't understand," she says, shaking her head slowly.

I haul the Bard Box up onto her table. It has limited memory, but it should have picked up a good few seconds before cutting off. Checking over both my shoulders to make sure no one else is around, I press the play button.

*"What if someone finds it?"*

The voices are muffled and distant, but I can make out the words clearly. Oh, Bard Box, you clever, clever thing.

*"They're not gonna find it. Only a few people even* know *about the clubhouse."*

*"Why wouldn't you just destroy it?"*

Frodo quacks, and the recording cuts off. My heart is racing.

"Damn, Henderson," says Eddie. "I leave you alone for fifteen minutes and you've done a whole sting operation?"

"It's nothing, really," I say, bashful, but Eddie holds out a hand for a high five, and I eagerly accept, slapping his palm with mine.

Anika frowns at the Bard Box, then lifts her gaze to mine and Danny's in turn. She sniffles, looking lost. "And . . . you guys want to help me?"

"Of course we do," says Danny, putting a comforting hand on her shoulder.

"We want to put a stop to this sabotage and this curse," I say. "The fair's integrity as a competition is at risk. This is bigger than just one plant. But if your plant's out there, we'll find it."

Eddie interjects, joining our circle from where he's been lingering a safe distance from Danny and Frodo, who's waddling around on his leash.

"Listen, far be it from me to narc on someone," he says,

"but don't you think this is something we should let the adults handle? You guys have audio evidence that someone's messing with stuff—"

"It's not enough," Anika says. "They won't believe us unless we have something solid, or they'll just think we did it ourselves. Who's to say our projects didn't fail, and we're just trying to save face?"

"Anika's right," I say. "We can't go to the judges until we know who's responsible."

Eddie shrugs and puts his hands up as if to say *leave me out of it* and backs out of the huddle, warily eyeing Frodo, who's now pecking at Danny's shoelace.

"Which means it's up to us!" Danny says. "This is so *cool*!"

Anika cuts Danny a glare.

"Uh, s-sorry, not to say what happened to you is *cool*," Danny stutters. "Just, I've never been part of a whodunit like this before."

Anika's glare wavers and wiggles into something nearing a smile, the first glimmer of one I've seen from her.

"I guess I haven't either," she says. But her smile fades quickly. "It's just . . . the stakes are high for me. I'm on scholarship at Eastwood Academy *because* of fairs like this and—if I put this dead plant out there, I could lose everything."

"Then we'd better get moving," I say. "We'll get to the *root* of this plant problem." I grin and raise my brows. Eddie groans. "Come on, the *root*?"

Danny laughs but covers his mouth with his hand

apologetically when Anika pointedly does not laugh.

"Anyway"—I clear my throat—"do you recognize either of the voices on the recording? Or do you know what 'the clubhouse' is?"

"No, I—I mostly keep to myself," says Anika. "I don't have a lot of friends at Eastwood."

I think that translates to an admission that she's almost as much of a loser at Eastwood Academy as I am at Hawkins High.

"Yeah, we're newbies here, so we're not much better," says Danny.

"I met a guy earlier," I say. "He seemed to know a lot about the regional science fair circuit. He was a sabotage victim a few years ago. Maybe he knows something?"

"I'm hesitant to trust *anyone* right now," Anika says. "Are you sure we want to bring in more people?"

"Do we have any better ideas?" I ask.

"We could always divide and conquer and search the convention center for this clubhouse," Danny says.

"The Indiana Convention Center has fifty-five meeting rooms, five exhibition halls, and two grand ballrooms," Anika says, like she's reciting from a brochure. "It would take us ages to search everywhere, and that's assuming they hid it *inside* the convention center and not somewhere else nearby."

Danny winces. I don't need to calculate those odds to know that they're not great.

"Then Brian it is," I say.

"I think you're right," Anika sighs, like the admission pains her. "Let's go."

"You don't have to if you don't want to," says Danny. "We can handle this and let you know as soon as—"

"It's my project they've targeted," Anika says. "It's *me* they've picked a fight with. I won't take that sitting down."

Danny's smile brightens; he's dazzled by Anika's determination. I turn to Eddie as I pick up the Bard Box.

"Eddie, you should stay here and keep watch for anything else suspicious," I say. "You can make sure no one messes with Frodo."

"Oh, you are *not* making me babysit the *duck,*" Eddie protests.

"It's just for fifteen minutes, dude," I say. "Think of it as an opportunity to face your fears!" Robin would be so proud of me.

"Oh, for the love of—" Eddie throws his hands up in the air and looks at the ceiling like he'd like to have a word with the man upstairs about this situation. Once no sign from God makes itself apparent, he points at me in a way that might feel more threatening from a man unafraid of ducks. "You *owe* me, Henderson."

Danny gives Frodo's leash to Eddie with a smile.

"Be good, Frodo," Danny says.

"He'd better," Eddie grumbles.

Eddie glares down at the duck, and that's how we leave them—in the middle of an intense staring contest. I can only hope they don't kill each other.

▶

We search the expo hall to no avail before we delve into the lobby and the sponsor exhibits. I wanted to check out the sponsor tables anyway, so I'm happy to take in all of the cool science displays as we search the area.

There are booths from all sorts of technology and science companies, from traditional labs to big corporations to video game programmers and everything in between. There are local and regional science and technology organizations for students, and countless schools recruiting for science programs, both at the collegiate level and at the high school level. There are all sorts of gimmicks, games, and freebies to draw people in, like wheels to spin and trivia to play in exchange for rewards. It's all fun, and futuristic, and exciting.

But Brian isn't anywhere to be seen.

"Do you see him?" Anika asks.

"Not yet," I say, still scanning the room.

"Ooh, free pens!" Danny says, darting over to some energy company's table to sift through their freebie basket.

I give Anika an apologetic smile. "He's, uh, distractible," I say.

"It's okay," says Anika. "It's cute." Immediately, her eyes widen and her face flushes, like she hadn't meant to say that out loud. She clears her throat and ducks toward the nearest booth as a distraction.

I follow her and find us at a table for Eastwood Academy,

the school Brian and Anika go to that specializes in science and technology, and whatever teasing I had ready for Anika dies on my tongue. The display has a rolling TV cart set up to play footage of what I assume is the campus, which is gorgeous and modern and sleek, filled with high-end facilities, and grand, expansive labs. I watch wide-eyed as the video plays and then loops back to the beginning. It all seems unreal. I'm used to Hawkins, with its hand-me-down textbooks and ancient, outdated lab equipment.

I pick up a pamphlet that's full of photos of smiling students. What must it be like, to go to a school that *cares* about knowledge and curiosity? I imagine it would be like I felt when I got here, to the science fair, or the way I feel during summers at Camp Know Where. Like I'm surrounded by energy and passion and *possibility.*

"Hey, if you're curious about Eastwood Academy, or have any questions, I'm here to help," says the man behind the table. He's got a handlebar mustache and is wearing a bow tie and head-to-toe tweed.

"I don't know," I say, putting the pamphlet back. "Just daydreaming."

"Why just daydreaming?" Mustache Man asks. "If you're here today, you clearly care about science. And Eastwood is the place to be for people who work tirelessly in exploring science and technology."

"I believe you," I say. "I'm just not interested in switching schools."

"Well, if you change your mind, just say the word," says

Mustache Man, and turns his attention to another student.

Anika sways toward me like she's curious, but isn't sure she's allowed to ask. Finally, she dares:

"I didn't know you were interested in Eastwood," she says, curiosity tinging her voice.

"Just in that it sounds like nerd heaven," I say. "You go there, right?"

"Yes," she says. "It's nice in some ways. They really care about empowering students to make an impact. . . ."

She trails off, and I push—

"But . . . ?"

She shrugs. "But nowhere is perfect. Even here, there's a vandal lurking. There are hateful people everywhere."

"Yeah, I guess," I say. I think my hypothesis that she's a bit of a loser, like I am, might be correct. But it's hard to imagine a school full of nerds being hateful in the way that Hawkins can be hateful, and certainly not to someone who's as much of a genius as Anika clearly is.

I tear myself away from the idyllic images of science and academia and turn back to the rest of the fair, just as Danny reappears at Anika's side.

"I got two pens, a tote bag, and a koozie," he says, proudly showing off his haul.

I don't look at his goodies, because I'm too busy spotting Brian chatting with a company representative at one of the booths.

"I have eyes on the target," I tell Danny. "Three o'clock."

Danny's face screws up in confusion. "That'll be too

late, the first group's judging is at noon."

"Three o'clock as in to your right, dude," I say, rolling my eyes.

"Oh." Danny whips around.

"Just, uh," I say, "follow my lead?"

I march forward with as much confidence as I can muster, Danny and Anika on my heels. Brian says goodbye to the company rep and steps away from the booth. He spots us approaching, and his eyebrows shoot up, one hand lifting in an uncertain wave, his face devoid of any trace of enthusiasm.

"Hey, Brian," I say, coming to a stop in front of him. He's flipping a tidy folder of résumés closed, the picture of professionalism in his jacket and tie.

"Dustin, right?" he says. "Getting some essential networking in, I'm guessing?"

"Not quite," I say.

"You should," he says. "It's never too early to start. I've been working some of these relationships since I was a freshman. You'll thank me when you're a senior."

"Yes. Totally. I will get right on that," I rush out. "But first, I was actually hoping we could ask you something. About the, uh, the curse."

"Oh," says Brian, surveying our ragtag little group. His gaze lingers on Anika. "I heard you got hit this year, Anika. I know how much that sucks."

"Yeah," she says. "It does."

"That's why we're here," I say. "We have reason to

believe her plant is still out there, and we're doing whatever we can to get it back."

"What?" Brian says, voice gone squeaky. "How?"

Danny leans in, looking both ways to make sure no one else is within earshot. "Can you keep a secret?" he asks.

Brian looks stricken, but says, "Of course."

I've got the Bard Box at my side, and I glance around the crowded sponsors' area warily.

"Maybe somewhere a little quieter?" I suggest.

Brian shoves his hands in his pockets and takes a step backward. "Look, I hate the curse as much as anyone, and I truly hope you get your plant back, but this is a vital time to make connections, for my future. Whatever has happened here, I cannot afford to interrupt what I came here to do."

God, Eddie was right about Brian being a bit of a tool. But he seems really tapped into the science fair's gossip network, and we desperately need intel, so I resist the urge to call him out on it.

"We'll keep it quick," I promise.

Brian doesn't look convinced, but when I nod my head to the side in a *follow me* gesture, he relents and joins us in a quieter corner, away from the hustle and bustle.

We circle around the Bard Box, and I look from face to face with a grave warning: "What I'm about to show you is top secret information, do you understand? You can't breathe a word of this to anyone or our whole investigation is compromised."

Brian arches an eyebrow and looks between me, Danny, and Anika in bemused disbelief.

"Come on, how serious can it be?" he asks. He lets out a laugh that feels very much at our expense.

"*Deadly* serious," I say, with a tone that matches my words.

Brian rolls his eyes and lifts his hands, palms up. "Okay, okay. Show me, then."

I exchange wary glances with Anika and Danny, checking if any of them have objections to sharing, and when they don't, I press the button to play the recording.

*"What if someone finds it?"*

Brian's expression remains carefully neutral as the voices on the recording crackle to life, and I watch his face in anticipation.

*"They're not gonna find it. Only a few people even know about the clubhouse."*

*"Why wouldn't you just destroy it?"*

Frodo's quack signals the end of the recording. We're all silent for a long moment as Brian processes the information. His jaw is rippling as he thinks, and it's all I can do not to shout at him to tell us everything he knows, *now.*

"Where did you hear this?" he finally asks.

Danny says, "The expo hall, during the opening address."

"I know you know a lot of people," I say. "At least the Eastwood crowd. Do you recognize the voices? Or, do you know where this 'clubhouse' is? We're trying to save Anika's project before the judging starts and we don't have many leads."

"God, I wish I could help more," Brian says. "But . . . I have no idea what the clubhouse is. I've never heard of it before. It could be anywhere in Indianapolis, for all we know."

My stomach sinks.

"I'm done for, aren't I?" Anika says, already devolving back into panic.

"No way," says Danny, squeezing her shoulder. "We're gonna find it, Anika!"

"What about the voices?" I press. "Do you recognize either of them?"

Brian frowns and he shakes his head. "I don't know. . . . It's hard to tell with the distortion."

Brian studies me for a long moment and then chews on the inside of his cheek.

"But if I had to guess," he says, slow, thoughtful, "I mean, I'm *really* not certain about this, but, shot in the dark? The bossy guy sounds like this kid in my chem class, maybe? Richard, his name is. He has that same nasally tone."

"Okay," I breathe, granted even the slightest hint of hope. "Okay, where can we find this Richard? What's he look like?"

Brian scans the room like he's hoping Richard is around

somewhere, but sees nothing of note.

"He, uh, has short, dark hair. I haven't seen him today, but he's gotta be around here somewhere. Rasch, I think, is his last name, if you want to ask around."

"Right. Okay," I say. Any lead is better than what we have, which is a whole lot of nothing. A name is a good start. "We'll try to track him down."

"And thanks, seriously!" Danny says.

"Yeah, thank you," Anika says, a bit less enthusiastically. "I know we're not exactly friends. . . ."

"Of course," says Brian. "I of all people know what it's like to see your project fail so close to the finish line. I hope you find the guy, really."

Figures that the status-obsessed kid would be interested in vengeance, of all things.

"Now I need to get back to schmoozing these recruiters, okay?" Brian says. "But good luck."

Without further ado, Brian scurries back to the expo hall, leaving me, Danny, and Anika with the Bard Box and a name: Richard Rasch.

"Okay," Anika says. "It's a lead, at least."

"Yeah," I agree. "I want to drop the Bard Box off with Eddie, but then we can ask around and find this guy."

"And we gotta work fast," Danny says. "We've only got half an hour till judging starts."

▶

There's a decent-size crowd of students forming around my booth when we return to the expo hall.

"What's going on?" Danny asks.

"No clue," I say.

As we draw closer, I realize Eddie is at the center of the crowd, gesticulating wildly despite holding Frodo's leash in one hand. The students lean in, hanging on his every word, and it's not hard to see why: Eddie's in full Dungeon Master mode.

"And when the man went back into the house," he says, "there, on his coat, right where the woman had grabbed him . . . was a *handprint,* burned into the fabric."

The crowd lets out a collective gasp, and immediately kids start crying out in protest.

"No way!" a boy says. "But the woman wasn't real!"

"Oh, but who are *we* to decide what's real?" Eddie asks with a grin as he looks at the chaos he's unleashed in the form of a dozen terrified science nerds.

"Oh my God, oh my God," says a girl, covering her ears with her hands. "I'm going to have nightmares."

Eddie looks over the crowd and sees us and his spine straightens as he clears his throat. He almost looks embarrassed, like we've caught him—doing what, I'm not sure.

"Anyways, story time's over, little twerps, scurry along," he says.

The group lets out disappointed noises, groans and

*awww*s, but Eddie just waves them off with a shooing motion.

"Mr. Eddie," says a girl who looks far too young to be participating in a high school science fair, but maybe she skipped a few grades. "Will you tell us more stories later after the judging's over?"

"I'll consider it," Eddie says. "But only if you absolutely *nail* your presentation, okay?"

"Okay," the girl says, giving Eddie a sweet smile. "Bye, Mr. Eddie! Bye, Mr. Quackins!"

She disperses with the rest of the crowd, which allows me to stroll over to Eddie with raised eyebrows.

*"Mr. Eddie?"* I ask, incredulous. "What was all that about?"

An hour ago, people were avoiding Eddie like the plague. Now they're gathered around him for campfire stories? Leave it to Eddie to charm half the convention center in a few hours.

"Oh, nothing, just some kids told me I was scary. So I thought I'd give them something to *really* be scared of." He grins. "Didn't expect to gather such a crowd."

"Frodo didn't give you too much trouble, did he?" asks Danny, darting forward to scoop up the duck and press a kiss to his head.

"Neither of us killed each other," Eddie says. "I'll count that as a win."

"Good," I say, "because we need you to duck-sit a little while longer."

Eddie closes his eyes and exhales, like he's trying to keep calm. "Dude, I'm trying to give you space to do your thing," he says, "but you are *really* testing my limits here."

"Eddie, you *know* my friends are coming even though things have been weird with us, and I want to impress them. And now we've got"—I check my watch—"T-minus twenty-two minutes to find the plant and get it back to Anika's booth before judging starts."

"Oh my God," Anika groans, clutching her stomach like the reminder pains her.

"And I need to know that the Bard Box—and, yes, *the duck*—are safe while we go track down Richard."

"Who the hell is Richard?" Eddie asks.

"The culprit, dude, keep up!" I say. I turn to Anika and Danny. "I hate to say it, but we need to split up to cover more ground. Do you guys have walkie-talkies on you?"

"Why would we have walkie-talkies with us?" Anika asks.

I roll my eyes. *Amateurs.* I guess we can't all be trained adventurers.

"Okay, fine, then we'll just—meet up here in ten minutes, whether we've found Richard or not, okay? Let's synchronize our watches."

"Wow," Danny breathes. "I've never had reason to synchronize my watch with anyone before."

"Yeah, thrilling stuff," Eddie says.

As I check that our watches match up, I quickly formulate a plan to divide and conquer.

"Danny, you stick around here in the expo hall," I say. "Anika, you tackle the sponsors' area. I'll go scope out the lobby."

"On it!" Danny says, giving me a dead serious salute until he can't hold back his smile anymore. With a slightly crazed grin, he scurries off.

"What if we can't find him, Dustin?" Anika asks. "What's the plan then?"

"We'll figure it out," I tell her. "I promise. We're going to get to the bottom of this."

Not just for Anika, I don't say, but for *me*. Because I need to impress my friends if they're coming all this way to see me, and I'm pretty sure the Bard Box, awesome as it is, isn't going to win me any prizes. No, this mystery is my only chance to show Mike and Lucas that I can do awesome things all by myself. Because they seem more than happy to be on their own. I have to show them I am too.

"Okay," Anika says. "I'll see you back here. Hopefully with Richard in tow."

She rushes off toward the lobby. I hesitate for only a moment, and then I'm off too.

▶

I've spent all of five minutes asking around for Richard before I start to suspect this is a waste of time.

No one seems to know the guy, not even the kids I've talked to who go to Eastwood Academy. A few people even laugh when I ask, like there's some sort of joke I'm not privy to, like maybe Richard is notoriously difficult to get ahold of or something. I'm starting to feel a bit hopeless as the meetup time approaches.

I'm in the middle of the lobby, an absolute storm of activity around me in every direction as people prepare for the first judging period. Everyone is running to and from the expo hall, projects in tow. I've been so preoccupied with the mystery of the saboteurs that I've forgotten to be nervous about the judging, but I can only imagine how Anika must feel without a project to present. I take in my surroundings, trying to find my next target to ask about Richard. A girl in one corner, crying to her mom about something or other. A group of friends laughing loudly over some game. A boy being scolded by a janitor for littering right next to a trash can.

And that sight—the janitor with her rolling cart of trash and cleaning supplies—makes me think that maybe we've been going about this all wrong.

Because we want to find Richard so we can find the clubhouse. But maybe Richard is *in* the clubhouse. Maybe we don't need Richard to find the clubhouse, maybe it's the other way around. The guys we overheard said only a few people knew about the clubhouse—but if anyone were to know about a secret hideout in the convention center, it would be the person responsible for cleaning it up.

I beeline over to the janitor, who's replacing the bag in a trash can.

"Hi there, uh, Miss Janitor," I say, mustering up my most brownnosing, ass-kissing smile. "Do you have a minute?"

The janitor is old and wrinkled and completely unimpressed.

"Oh, I've got nothing but time," she deadpans. "Just cleaning up after a thousand teenagers who don't know how to get their trash in the garbage can. What do you want?"

Okay, not the warmest welcome. But I can make it work. She might not be receptive to me asking directly, but maybe I just need to soften her up first.

Luckily, I'm an expert flatterer.

"Ma'am," I say, layering my words with my most genuine charm and appreciation. "I just wanted to say how much I appreciate your work in making this event possible."

The woman snorts, not buying it, and continues replacing the trash bag, grumbling under her breath. I could change tactics—but instead, I double down.

"Seriously," I say. "I mean it. This whole thing is made possible by people like you. If this event is a voyage of curiosity, then *you* are the current, or the tide. The invisible force that enables people like me to set sail on the ocean of knowledge. And I don't think you get enough appreciation for that."

The woman eyes me suspiciously, and I work hard to keep my smile bright and earnest under her scrutinizing gaze. Slowly but surely, her icy glare thaws, and her mouth twitches into a self-satisfied smile.

"You know, you're right, kid," she says. "Thanks for saying so."

My heart races as I realize that this is my opportunity. I try not to seem too eager, forcing myself to be casual.

"Of course," I say. "I mean, all this event space must be hard to maintain. And that's not even counting all the areas that aren't publicly available, like, the clubhouse."

It's a shot in the dark, and I bite my lip, waiting for a response.

"Oh, tell me about it," grouches the woman. "Those kids always leave that room wrecked."

My heart skips a beat. *There it is.*

"It's *so* inconsiderate," I agree emphatically. "In fact, I was just thinking about heading to the clubhouse to clean up at least a little so you won't have so much to deal with later. The only thing is, I, uh, kind of forgot the room number."

"Oh, you don't have to do that, kid," says the woman. "I complain about you kids, but it's my job, after all."

"Yeah, of course," I say, "but that doesn't mean we shouldn't make it easier for you. Do you mind reminding me where the clubhouse is? So I can just, uh, do some trash collection? For you and your colleagues. Really, it would make me feel a *lot* better."

The woman narrows her eyes. "I know those Eastwood kids are pretty protective about that clubhouse," she says.

"Yeah, totally," I say, nodding rapidly. "That's why, you know, it's up to me, if I want to keep it clean! Because the other kids who know about it just don't care about the—the hardworking staff of the convention center and making their lives easier. And it'd be *so* embarrassing for me to have to ask my friend the room number again. Maybe you could remind me?"

She looks at me for a beat, and I think I've been too obvious, that she's onto me, that she's going to tell me to get lost and leave her to do her job in peace. But then she shrugs, like she really couldn't care less.

"Sure, kid, whatever," she says. "It's room 143. And look, if you're gonna clean up, keep the recycling and the trash separate, okay? If you really care about making my life easier."

"Yes! Of course!" I say, trying to keep my enthusiasm from bubbling over in a way that might be suspicious, but it's hard, because inside I'm jumping for joy and tempted to run around the convention center whooping like I'm doing a victory lap. "I really appreciate it—and your janitorial work. We'd all be lost without you!"

And with that, just as my watch flickers to the time when I'm supposed to head back to meet with Danny and Anika, I shoot the janitor lady a big grin and a thumbs-up, and I sprint off toward the expo hall.

▶

I'm rushing toward the table, where Anika and Danny are waiting with Eddie and Frodo. They look dejected. Anika has her arms crossed over her chest while Danny pats her shoulder and consoles her.

They look up as I skid to a stop in front of them, and I don't bother with pleasantries or checking how their searches went, because we have eight minutes until judging, and we can't waste a second of it.

"Everybody settle down and shut up," I say. "I know where the clubhouse is. I've got a plan, but it'll only work if you *all* listen closely and do *exactly* as I say. From here on out, every moment counts."

Frodo quacks. Eddie flinches. Anika looks seconds from tears. Danny just looks up at me expectantly, ready and awaiting orders.

We have less than ten minutes. But if the plan I have in mind works, time won't be an issue. If the plan I have in mind works, everything will be just fine.

"Okay," I say. "Let's save this plant. It's time for a goddamn heist."

# CHAPTER NINETEEN

## SATURDAY, DECEMBER 7, 1985
## 11:57 A.M.

The plan is simple, but we have to execute it perfectly. We all need to be back at our booths in time for judging, but especially Anika, whose scholarship on the line, so she'll be staying put, ready to go whether we find her plant or not. Luckily, we have a secret weapon: Eddie, who is on diversion duty. His job is to delay the judging by any means necessary, to buy me and Danny time to break into the clubhouse, get the plant, and get it back before judging. Eddie had an evil kind of grin when he received his assignment, which I choose not to think too deeply about for the sake of my sanity, if not for plausible deniability.

But really, if all goes according to plan, it should be easy.

Anika heads to the expo hall and her booth, and Danny and I head to seek out room 143, Frodo waddling along ahead of us on his leash.

I'm sure we stick out even more than Eddie did since we're the only people going against the current, moving away from the expo hall while all the other students steadily pour into it, heading toward their booths for judging. I can only hope Eddie buys us enough time to get back for our own judging.

According to the convention center map, the room we're looking for is on the edge of the building, in a wing that's closed off during the science fair. Which means we're venturing into uncharted territory.

The farther we get from the expo hall, the emptier the hallways of the convention center become. Most every student in the building should be in the hall for judging, with friends and family waiting anxiously in the lobby, leaving only those of us on a mission to wander the halls.

Finally, Danny and I reach the right wing, and I count off the meeting rooms as we pass them.

"One-thirty-seven . . . one-thirty-nine . . . one-forty-one . . ." We skid to a stop in front of room 143. "And—crap."

There's a lockbox on the door, which sets it apart from every other one we've passed. I grab the lockbox, peer closer, and see that it has a four-letter code. I try the door handle. It's definitely and hopelessly *locked*.

But there are words written neatly on the lockbox—

"You can't see me, but I can see you," Danny reads, voice strained. "To be more specific, I see through."

"What am I?" We read the last part together.

"A riddle," I say.

"We could always just knock," Danny suggests.

"If we have any luck at all, that room will be empty," I say. "But if it isn't and we knock, we'd just be warning them to destroy the plant, or sneak out the window, or something else." I squint, looking closer at the words on the lockbox. "No. No, we can do this."

*You can't see me, but I can see you.*

Binoculars, maybe, or a telescope?

"A ghost, maybe?" Danny says.

I squeeze my eyes shut, trying to focus, the image of the words on the note burned into the backs of my eyelids.

*To be more specific, I see through.*

A two-way mirror? But it needs to be a four-letter code . . . unless the note is a warning that we're being watched.

I can't help but look around, like there might be a hidden camera or something waiting to be discovered. But it's just us, and the riddle.

"Maybe it's something to do with sound waves . . . ," Danny says.

You can't see me, but I can see you.

I see *through*.

What am I?

*"Boom!"* I shout and grab the lockbox again.

Quickly but carefully, I scroll the dials to each letter—X-R-A-Y.

The lockbox clicks open.

"Good lord, you're a genius!" Danny says.

I gesture to my T-shirt—germanium, nickel, uranium, sulfur. "I've been *saying* that."

The key in the lockbox shakes right out into my palm, and I swiftly press it into the lock, twisting it until it clicks. I turn the handle and it yields, the door swinging open to reveal—

What was once an ordinary meeting room has been decked out from floor to ceiling to the best of a high schooler's ability. A shag rug looks like it's seen better days, but there's a soda fountain in one corner with an array of Coke products, a counter with a coffee machine and fixings, a projector set up with a line of bulky massage chairs facing the screen, and a coffee table stacked high with board games and littered with empty pizza boxes. It's no Palace Arcade, but for a hideout in a convention center, it's pretty swanky.

There's someone sitting in a massage chair at the center of the lineup, feet propped up on the coffee table, headphones connected to a Walkman over his ears, a drink in one hand, a lit cigarette in the other.

The guy jolts up at our entrance and shoves the headphones off his ears, regarding us with wide eyes above his handlebar mustache and polka-dot bow tie.

It's the Eastwood Academy representative from the booth earlier. Mustache Man. Except that buttoned-up, straitlaced guy seems far from the person in front of us. Literally, in some ways, as his bow tie has been tugged loose so that he could undo a few buttons of his shirt.

"Wh—" The guy scrambles to set down his drink and hastily stub out his cigarette. He nearly trips over himself as he jolts to his feet from the massage chair, which continues to whir and shake. "This area is off-limits. Shouldn't you be on the main floor for judging?"

My eyebrows shoot up. "Shouldn't *you*?" I ask.

"I— You—!" Mustache Man sputters. Then, "Is that a duck?"

Danny is nicer than I am for not calling him out for asking such an obvious question.

"But where's the plant?" he asks instead.

And I realize he's right. I don't see it anywhere. Not good.

"What plant?" demands Mustache Man.

I charge forward, ignoring his indignant grunts of outrage, to look under the coffee table, inside the cabinets under the coffee bar setup, and—

Squished under the sink, slightly bent but still very much alive, is Anika's superplant.

"Wow," Danny breathes behind me.

I shoot a glare over my shoulder at Mustache Man, who

is hovering in front of the door with a general aura of disgruntled disdain.

"Do you think we're stupid?" I ask. "There's no way your students have been using this room to sabotage projects and you don't know about it."

Mustache Man sputters again. He's a collection of noises I've never heard before. It almost makes me want to get him in a room with the Bard Box.

"I assure you I know *nothing* of sabotage!" he manages at last.

I hoist the plant up and out of the cupboard. Danny crowds in to gently fluff up its leaves and straighten its stem.

"I've just—had a *very* long day," Mustache Man continues. "So yes, when I can sneak away for a moment, I use the Eastwood students' hideout that they think I don't know about. But it's harmless! And there's a soda machine! And, good God, where did they get these massage chairs? But *cheating*? In this vital institution of knowledge? Well, I *never*."

"Look, sir, with respect?" I say, valiantly resisting the urge to roll my eyes. "We're on a time-sensitive mission here to recover this plant from a serial saboteur who may or may not be named Richard."

"And you think it's someone from Eastwood?" the man asks. Understanding seems to finally dawn on him, and he looks at the plant with horror. "This is *serious*. There should be consequences—"

"Yes, there should," I say. "And if you're serious about that, then you can find me at booth 403 after the judging period is done. But for now, the clock is ticking."

I glance at my watch. God, I hope Eddie's pulled through with a delay. I stare down the teacher, who's still in front of the door, challenging him, *daring* him to stop us.

"So are you going to stand on the side of injustice and the academic fraud that happened under your nose?" I ask. "Or are you going to *stand aside* and let us return this plant to its rightful owner, and make things right?"

Sheepishly, the man steps aside.

A rush of excitement surges through me, and I feel light as air, like I'm floating down the hallway as Danny and I leave the clubhouse and Mustache Man behind. Because we have the plant! We're going to get it to Anika in time for judging! We'll find and confront Richard, and the day will be saved. We'll be heroes!

We move as quickly as we can with me weighed down by Anika's plant. When Frodo's waddling proves too slow, Danny scoops him up.

I skid to a halt when we reach the lobby. There's not a student in sight, and the expo hall doors are closed.

The judging has started.

A sinking feeling blooms in my stomach and slow steps pull me to the doors. I yank at the door handles. They don't budge. We're too late.

Except, the doors suddenly burst open. I nearly drop

Anika's plant as I scramble out of the way, just as two men haul a guy out by his arms.

"Gentlemen, if you wanted an excuse to feel my arms you could have just asked—" And then Eddie's stumbling out into the lobby like he's been shoved. He catches his balance. "Jeez, go easy! Whatever happened to hospitality?"

The two men glare at him and go back into the expo hall.

Hope explodes inside my chest.

"Eddie!" I exclaim.

"It's about damn time you showed up," Eddie says. He grins at me, then leaps forward to catch one of the doors by its handle just before it clicks shut.

"What the hell did you do?" I hiss, equal parts concerned and impressed.

"Nothing illegal," he says, waving a hand dismissively. "But we'll debrief later. They've started judging. You might need to improvise to get that plant to Anika without drawing attention to yourselves."

"A stealth mission," I say. "Copy that."

*"Copy that,"* Danny repeats reverently. "I've always wanted to say that."

"Stick to the shadows, my friends," Eddie says. I think he means *good luck.*

Either way, I nod once, determined. And with that, Danny and I enter the expo hall.

The huge room is just as full of projects as it was earlier, just as bursting with curious students, but now there's a thick blanket of anxiety over it all. Students aren't chatting with their neighbors, aren't even fiddling with their projects or rehearsing their presentations. They stand and wait in anticipation as the judges make their way through the hall, one five-minute presentation at a time.

The judges are at the far side of the room, still on the first row of projects. While they don't notice our entrance, a few students near us whip around with glares.

Anika's and my booths are just one row down from where the judges are. Which means we *really* don't have much time to pull this off.

I lower myself so that I'm concealed by the line of trifold poster boards and gesture for Danny to do the same.

We creep a few steps down, but stealth is not easy when encumbered by a superplant. It's heavy, and its offensively large leaves are not exactly discreet as they peek up over the cover of the posters. I might as well be a walking tree, and the students nearby are shooting us dirty looks of varying intensity.

I peek at the judges' progress. They're only a few spots down from Anika now. There's no way we can get to her booth without the judges noticing us. We need to get their attention away from Anika just long enough to get her the plant and take our spots at our booths.

That's when I spot the girl with the lawn-mowing contraption that is, for all intents and purposes, a Barbie car armed with knives. I stop in my tracks suddenly enough that Danny runs into me and Frodo lets out a little quack.

I turn toward them slowly, the gears in my head turning so rapidly I feel like there should be steam coming out of my ears.

"Frodo," I whisper the name like a revelation as a new plan begins to form. "Of course."

Because we need a distraction, and Frodo is a very talented duck.

"What?" Danny asks. "What's the plan?"

It's not a plan so much as a Hail Mary, but it takes form in my mind, and it might just work.

"I need Frodo to cause chaos," I say. "You said he can open cage latches?"

I nod sharply toward the Barbie Knifemobile, which is rolling back and forth against the walls of its cage.

"Oh," breathes Danny, breaking into a grin, "he's been training his whole life for this."

Danny sets Frodo gently on the floor and unhooks the leash from his harness.

"We're gonna get closer," Danny whispers. "Stay here."

And with that, he and Frodo creep toward the Knifemobile, leaving me with the plant, waiting for the perfect opportunity.

Minutes seem to stretch into eternity as I peek over the posters and watch the judges inch closer and closer to Anika's booth. And mine. I glance toward Danny, who is still crouched and hiding a few yards from me, while Frodo ventures toward the Knifemobile's cage. He pecks curiously at the enclosure. For a second, I think we've overestimated the duck's ability and he's going to waddle off with no sense of urgency and no clue of what he's screwing up.

But then, Frodo nudges at the hooked latch, and it clicks open. And that's all he has to do, because the car is rolling forward, pushing the door open, and wheeling its way out onto the convention floor.

My breath catches in my chest. It worked—but only if the next part works too. If no one sees the Knifemobile, if panic doesn't electrify the crowd, then all we've done is set loose this poor girl's project for no reason.

Just as I'm thinking I may have miscalculated, someone lets out a bloodcurdling scream.

"What the hell is that?" someone asks.

*"KNIFE!"* someone else shouts. (To be precise, there are *multiple* knives. Semantics.)

And then everything falls apart, in the best way possible.

There's shrieking and shouting as people hop onto tables and run in all directions to put distance between themselves and the Knifemobile, which wheels along the floor with impressive speed. The judges—everyone in the expo hall, in fact—turn toward the commotion. I don't have any time to hesitate, I need to move.

I don't worry about being subtle now, because there's enough movement that I can blend in. I haul the plant past the last few rows of tables until I reach Anika's row. I peek again and see the judges aren't looking my way; they're all focused on the havoc a few rows over. The coast is clear— and I rush toward Anika with her plant.

Her face lights up when she sees me and the gargantuan tomato plant in my arms. I flash her a sunny smile as I heave the plant onto her table, unceremoniously shoving the dead plant from its place. It falls to the ground behind the table, out of sight, like it never even existed.

"You did it," Anika breathes. Bewildered, she looks in the direction of the havoc caused the unleashed Knifemobile. "Did you have something to do with this?"

"Not in a way that can be proved," I say, grinning as I slide into my spot in front of my booth, where the Bard Box waits. "No further problems?"

"All seems well," Anika says. "No one went near your project but me and Brian."

Brian is on the other side of my booth with his water filtration system, hands clasped in front of him. He'd be the image of calm and focused if not for the tapping of his toes.

Across the hall, the shouting reaches a crescendo, and then everything comes to a stop. Danny leaps up, holding the Knifemobile like it's a fluffy friend and not a *car with knives duct-taped to it.*

"I got it!" he proclaims triumphantly.

As if he wasn't the one who unleashed it in the first place. I'm glad he prioritized making sure no one was harmed and that the car didn't get too far. I don't want to sabotage that girl's project for the sake of saving Anika's.

There's scattered, confused applause as the cause of the chaos is apprehended, and the girl rushes forward to take the Knifemobile from Danny's hands and ease it back into its cage. Danny dips down to scoop up Frodo, who seems to have been waiting patiently for the chaos to die down, and then he's rushing to his own booth just as the judges return to their places, only one spot down from Anika.

"Oh-*kay*," says one of the judges, whistling low under her breath. "With no further distractions, let's get back to it, shall we?"

The three judges return to the presentation at hand, and I catch my breath, still wound up with adrenaline. I can't believe we pulled it off. I'm giddy with satisfaction, and it's all I can do not to erupt with shocked laughter. Because, holy crap! We did it! We actually did it! We saved Anika's plant! And sure, we still have to find and confront Richard Rasch, but we're well on our way to saving the day!

The judges finish at the table and shift over to Anika's, and Anika begins her practiced spiel, demonstrating her plant in all its green glory. The judges nod enthusiastically, giving the plant impressed looks as they make notes on their clipboards.

But in the whirlwind of the heist, I forgot something very important: I have my own presentation to get through, and I've been so focused on helping Anika and the science fair as a whole that I barely rehearsed my presentation today.

My brain spins, and I look around helplessly. Anika is

giving the presentation of a lifetime, the judges listening thoughtfully. Brian is studying me with an inscrutable look on his face, likely preparing for his own presentation. A few aisles down, Danny is situating Frodo in his crate. Eddie will be out in the lobby along with the other friends and family not allowed on the floor during judging. Which means I'm on my own now. I had some allies in my solo quest, and Mike and Lucas could be arriving at any moment, but this part, only I can do. My heartbeat is reverberating in my head, my ears ringing, and then the judges are finishing their questions for Anika and turning their attention to me.

I swallow hard. This is it, then.

"Uh," I say. Which is never a good start. I clear my throat. "This is the Bard Box, a music-making machine."

I launch into the introduction I've ingrained in my brain over the last few months, having written and rewritten it and practiced it repeatedly both in my head and in front of a mirror. I explain what led to the Bard Box's invention and the scientific method framing the process—the hypotheses and datasets that show how awesome the Bard Box can be.

"But I think it's best if I just show you, and let you see for yourself," I say.

I turn to the Bard Box and press the button that has a prerecorded guitar riff courtesy of Eddie.

Except . . . nothing plays.

I glance sheepishly at the judges, who watch me with blank expressions, pens tapping against clipboards.

"Uh, sorry, I . . . ," I say, and I press the button again. *Nothing plays.*

I press the next button, which should have a drumbeat from Gareth. *Nothing.*

The next button should have a bass line from Doug. *Nothing.*

Desperate, I press the last button, which is programmed to play the most recent recording—the recording from this morning, of our suspects talking about getting rid of the plant.

Nothing.

Someone's erased everything.

It has to have been Richard. He must have found out we had a recording implicating him, and wanted to get rid of the evidence.

But how? The only people who know about the recording are people I trust. Eddie, who would never betray me. Danny, who was *there* when we made the recording. Anika and Brian, who were victims themselves.

I glance to my left. Anika is watching with anxious, wide eyes, and when she meets my gaze, she nods encouragingly.

I glance to my right. Brian isn't even looking in my direction.

But Brian had helped us, hadn't he? He'd told us about Richard Rasch—

Which had been a dead end.

Because—

Oh my God.

Richard Rasch?

As in—*Dick Rash?*

It was a fake name. Brian had wasted our time.

He'd told us he didn't know about the clubhouse, which was an Eastwood hideout, which he *had* to have known about, being as popular at Eastwood as he said he is.

But he'd been a victim of sabotage a few years ago, hadn't he? Or was that a lie to throw us off his tracks?

Because then, the way he'd panicked when I told him we thought the plant was still out there?

And, *son of a bitch,* the *recording*! The voice *had* sounded vaguely familiar, because it was *Brian*! I didn't recognize it because he'd only spoken briefly, but—

The judges stare at me expectantly and with growing concern, like they're worried I might be having a stroke. I am *also* slightly worried about that possibility.

Because Brian is the saboteur.

And I'm his latest victim.

"Uh," I say again, and clear my throat.

The judges don't know anything about the revelations I'm having. And they won't care. They only care about the Bard Box, which is next to me and completely devoid of music.

I don't have time to reel from my realization. I have to improvise. And I need to do it *now.*

Let the record show, I do not like singing in front of people aside from Suzie. But sometimes desperate times call for desperate measures.

I press the record button on the Bard Box.

*"Dun dun,"* I sing. *"Dun dun, dun dun, dun dun."*

The judges are looking at me like I'm insane. I might be. I finish the recording, set it to loop, and let my vocalized guitar riff set the tempo for the song.

For flair, I add the unmistakable, *"Ay, ay, ay."*

I hear people stifling laughter and exchanging whispers, but I don't have time to care. I push forward, press record, and add another layer of guitar riffs via *la-la-la*s. I set it to loop.

And I pray to the gods of metal that this works.

With the backing tracks set up, I open my mouth to sing.

"Crazy Train." Ozzy Osbourne. The ultimate solo quest.

I close my eyes against the watchful gaze of the judges and those of a hundred curious student onlookers, focusing on the music. I imagine I'm on the radio with Suzie, or in the car with Eddie, scream-singing along. And I let myself relax into the music, singing loud and proud, the Bard Box's backing loops carrying me through the first verse and the chorus.

And then I finish, clicking the button to turn off the Bard Box, and fall silent, regaining my breath.

There is no thunderous applause. There is no cheering. There are just three judges, stroking their chins and scribbling notes on their clipboards.

And then, one says, "Thank you for that."

They all turn to Brian's booth. Brian starts his speech to the judges. I watch, head spinning, thoughts running a mile a minute.

Because my presentation is over. Anika's project has been saved. But the case is far from closed.

Because Brian is the saboteur, and I need to prove it.

# CHAPTER TWENTY

## SATURDAY, DECEMBER 7, 1985
## 1:26 P.M.

Once the judging is over, we have a five-minute break before the exhibit hall opens and the public viewing starts. Leaving Frodo in his crate, Danny darts over from his booth to join me and Anika.

"Holy moly!" he says, practically vibrating with excitement. "That was intense! I can't believe we pulled that off!"

"We're not done yet," I warn.

"Yeah, I mean, what happened to your box?" Anika asks.

"I think," I say, "that our friend Brian might know the answer to that."

I speak loud enough so that Brian, only a few feet away at his booth, can hear the accusation. Danny lets out a dramatic gasp like my mom watching a plot twist on *Dynasty at the same time that* Anika and I turn to Brian.

Brian's eyes narrow and he crosses his arms in front of his chest. "Are you implying something?" he asks, accusatory.

"I don't get it," Danny says. "What about Richard Rasch?"

"It was a fake name," I tell him. "Dick Rash? *Real* creative. I'm embarrassed I didn't recognize it was fake earlier."

Screw it. I'm done playing games. There are no more heists to be had, no more investigations. It's time for the truth. All of it.

"You sabotaged my project," I say. "And Anika's. And who knows how many others!"

Brian's jaw drops, then opens and closes as he starts and stops a dozen protests.

"I don't know what you're talking about," is the defense he lands on.

"But what I don't understand," I continue like he hasn't spoken, "is why you would have sabotaged your own."

"I do," says Anika, realization dawning on her face, which is brightening with determination as she gets on the same page as me at lightning speed. "You were the first victim of the supposed curse, three years ago. But you weren't a *victim*, were you?"

Holy shit. Anika is right.

It's exactly the reason we were afraid to tell the teachers

or judges—we were afraid they'd think we had failed and were looking for excuses. Blaming curses and saboteurs for our own mistakes.

That's what Brian had done a few years ago.

"Your project choked," I say. "And instead of owning up to the fact that you messed up, you started sabotaging projects so you could blame the curse. I'm sure it didn't hurt to tackle the top competition—"

Brian scoffs. "How bold of you to assume *you're* top competition, coming here with your weird little music box and acting like science is *fun*? This stuff is *serious*. You have no idea what it's like. The pressure we're under!"

"Of all people, Brian, I can understand the pressure," Anika says. "But how does cheating help? All this will do is ruin your own life."

"Is that so?" Brian laughs. "You don't have any proof. Just an untested theory. And we *scientists* know that baseless theories are a dime a dozen."

And he's right, that we have no proof. He made sure of that.

Behind him, though, there is movement. Heading right toward us is Mustache Man from Eastwood Academy, one of the judges at his side, stern expressions on both their faces. I'd told Mustache Man to come by my booth after judging, and he's making good on that offer. My heart leaps into my throat as they draw near enough to hear Brian say—

"This is my last chance to win this stupid science fair

before college applications are due, and I'm not letting you Scooby-Doo wannabes stand in my way," he sneers. "I deleted your recording, and there's nothing you can do to prove I've done anything wrong."

I lift my chin in defiance and step forward, into his space, a challenge made bold by impending victory, like I've got a checkmate ready that we all know about but Brian.

"I don't know about that," I say. My eyes shift, pointedly, over his shoulder, and I address Mustache Man. "I mean, that confession seems like enough proof for a disqualification, don't you think?"

Brian whips around and is faced with Mustache Man and the judge standing there, listening with twin scowls directed right at him.

"What—? I—I—" Brian stutters. "I was—just joking. I didn't do anything. I don't even *know* this kid!"

The judge sighs and tucks her clipboard under her arm. "Let's make this easy, please? Just come with me and answer some questions, okay?"

"This is ridiculous!" Brian shouts, loud enough that he's drawing attention from nearby students who watch us curiously and then creep closer to eavesdrop. "You really believe this—this *random*? I go to *Eastwood Academy*! I'm a top student! My water filtration system is going to change the world!"

"Maybe," says the judge. "But it won't win this fair."

I muffle a snort of laughter by coughing into my hand.

Danny grabs my arm and shakes it like he can't contain his excitement, and from the corner of one eye I see Anika sag with relief.

Brian shoots us one last glare before his head drops and he allows the judge to lead him off, presumably to face the consequences of his actions.

And then he's gone, and it's just me with Anika and Danny on either side, facing Mustache Man, who is, aptly, twirling his mustache thoughtfully.

"Well, son of a dang *biscuit,* that was exciting!" Danny exclaims.

"I can't believe it," Anika breathes. "You did it. You actually did it."

"*We* did it," I correct.

It was Danny and Frodo who provided the distraction, and Anika who pieced together Brian's motive. I can't help but grin at Danny, who's positively wiggling with excitement.

Anika surges toward Mustache Man. "Thank you, Mr. Adams, seriously. I didn't think anyone would believe us."

"I almost didn't," admits Mustache Man, who apparently is Mr. Adams. "Or, I wouldn't have, if I hadn't seen your friends rescue the plant from right under my nose." He nods to Danny and me, then turns back to Anika. "A very impressive project, by the way. You are truly among Eastwood's brightest, and I hope you never forget that, certainly not on account of students like Brian."

Anika's eyes shine with tears like this means the world to her. "Thank you," she says.

"Now," says Mr. Adams, clapping his hands and facing me with focused intent. "Dustin, was it?"

I blink, surprised, and refrain from looking over my shoulder as if he could be speaking to someone else. "Uh, yeah, that's me."

"Do you mind if I talk to you alone for a moment?" he asks.

It takes me off guard a bit, and I worry I might not have avoided trouble completely. I had, after all, explored an off-limits section of the convention center and aided in setting that Barbie car loose to wreak havoc. But whatever the consequences, to me it was worth it.

"Sure," I say.

Mr. Adams and I step aside as Anika returns to her booth, and Danny casts me a double thumbs-up before darting back to his own booth where Frodo awaits. People are starting to pour in for the public viewing; guests are free to browse all of the projects while students give the same basic presentation over and over to small groups for an hour. Eddie should be back soon, and Mike and Lucas could be arriving any minute now, so I can't help but eagerly scan the crowds for them before turning my attention back to Mr. Adams.

"I know I wasn't supposed to find the clubhouse," I rush out. "And I know the knife-car thing was a drastic measure, but don't you think finding the culprit after years of sabotage counts for something?"

Mr. Adams's eyebrows arch. "I'm sorry, what?"

I blink. "Aren't I . . . in trouble?"

A beat passes with us staring blankly at each other.

"No, you aren't in trouble, I was just—" He breaks off. "The knife car was your doing?"

*Oops.* Clearly, he hadn't known that. Talk about shooting yourself in the foot.

I'm debating whether telling the truth or lying is the better way to go here. I don't want to get Danny in trouble, so maybe I can take all the blame, but—

"Actually, no," says Mr. Adams, before I can say anything. "I'm going to pretend I didn't hear that."

"I appreciate that," I say weakly. "But, if I'm not in trouble, what do you . . . ?"

Mr. Adams clears his throat, reaches up to tighten and straighten his bow tie and then smooths down his shirt. As if he's trying to impress *me.*

"I saw the end of your presentation," he says. "It was very impressive. And innovative. And—well, *fun.* In a way that is so often missing from science at Eastwood Academy."

"Uh, thanks?" I say. I'm still not sure where he's going with this, and I'm not yet convinced it doesn't end with me getting disqualified.

"I'm a recruiter," says Mr. Adams. "And if you want it, there's a spot for you at Eastwood."

I think my heart actually stops for a second. But that can't be possible, because that would kill me, and here I am standing, alive, even as I gape at Mr. Adams like a dead fish.

"I'd have to go through the proper channels, of course. But, assuming your grades are up to snuff, my word carries weight with the admissions committee," Mr. Adams goes on, oblivious to the short-circuiting in my brain. "We offer a collaborative working environment for students who are serious about science, engineering, and technology, and I think you could really thrive there. State-of-the-art facilities, a faculty with an impressive list of accolades and achievements. And bright students, such as yourself, of course."

"Holy shit," I say.

I wince, because I'm still so filled with adrenaline from the confrontation that I let myself forget he's an adult authority figure, around whom I should probably be watching my mouth. But Mr. Adams's mustache twitches like he's holding back a smile.

"Indeed," he agrees. "If money is an issue, I can put in a good word to the scholarship board, of course—"

"Holy *shit,*" I say again, decorum thrown to the wind, because this doesn't feel real. If I pinched myself, I'd still think I was dreaming.

I think of that video of Eastwood Academy with its shining labs and beautiful campus. I think of rigorous, challenging academics, industry-standard equipment, new opportunities. I think of going to school with people like Anika, who know that being smart—being a *nerd*—is cool.

I look up to see Eddie approaching from a few rows down. He lifts his hand in a wave.

And I think of my friends. I think of Mike and Lucas, who are coming all this way to support me, even if we haven't always seen eye to eye this year. I think of Max, who I haven't reached out to enough, after everything this summer. I think of Steve, and Robin, and Eddie. I think of my friends, and I can't help but think that there's nowhere I belong more than with them.

This was a solo quest, but ultimately, I don't know who I'd be without my party.

"I'm honored," I say. "Really. I mean, wow. But . . . I don't think Eastwood is for me. My place is in Hawkins. My friends are there."

"I'm sure your friends would want you to do what's best for your future," Mr. Adams says gently. "There's no pressure, but please, don't make any hasty decisions. If you have any questions—"

He conjures up a business card from the inside pocket of his tweed jacket and offers it to me. I take it in my hands, feeling the thick card stock.

"Just think about it, Dustin," Mr. Adams says. "Actually consider it. Okay?"

I nod shakily, not trusting myself to speak as my fingers curl around the business card. It feels like a betrayal even accepting it. But even as I agree to consider it, I think my decision is made.

"If you want to join us next year, you'll need to reach out before the new year," Mr. Adams says. "I hope to hear from you."

He gives me a last encouraging smile before he walks away.

I watch him head off to chat with another student at their booth, and I feel a little numb. Like I don't know *how* to feel, so my body has decided the right answer is *nothing*. Or maybe I've used up all my emotional energy for the day and this is what I'm left with.

"That man looks like a cartoon character," says Eddie, sidling up to me. "What was that about?"

"Uh, he was just—" I start. Then stop. I shove the business card into my pocket. Out of sight, out of mind. "Nothing. It was nothing."

"Well, jeez, dude, how did judging go?" he pushes. "Give me *something* here!"

I brighten, shaking away thoughts of that absurd, terrifying offer to focus instead on all the other excitement of the day.

"Dude, you missed *everything*," I say. "We solved the mystery! We caught the bad guy!"

"You found him?"

"Turns out it was *Brian*," I say. "You were totally right when you clocked him as a jerk earlier."

"I always knew I had a sixth sense for douchebaggery," Eddie says.

"I had to completely improvise my demonstration with the Bard Box," I say. "I did 'Crazy Train'! It was awesome, you would have loved it!"

"Damn, kid, I'm proud of you!" Eddie says, dropping a hand on my head as if to ruffle my hair but only succeeding in setting my hat askew. I roll my eyes good-naturedly and tug the hat straight again. "That's one hell of a solo quest."

I shrug, a little bashful in the face of his enthusiasm. "It wasn't *quite* a solo quest, though," I say. "I mean, you, and Anika, and Danny—and Frodo! I couldn't have done any of it without you guys."

"Since when have you started embracing *modesty,* Henderson?" Eddie says. "Don't sell yourself short. You were the brains of the operation. Help or not, this was *your* quest."

I can't help the grin that spreads over my face. Eddie is right. It *was* my quest, and I kind of killed it. Innocents saved, monsters slain, treasure and experience points awaiting.

I can't wait to tell Mike and Lucas.

The first guests of the public viewing trickle toward my project, eyeing it curiously. Eddie graciously gestures toward me with a slight bow, like, *Take it away!* as he ducks out of the way.

I dive into my presentation and demonstration, explaining the project to each new group that makes its way to my station, but my attention is split as I'm keeping an eye out for Lucas and Mike with Nancy in tow.

Eddie politely peruses a few nearby projects, but mostly hovers and gives enthusiastic, thunderous applause each time I finish my presentation, which is both mortifying and satisfying in equal measures.

Mike and Lucas are running late at this point, but I'm not worried. There's still time left in the viewing period, and really, as long as they're here for the awards ceremony, that's the most exciting part.

Except, time keeps stretching on, and I keep giving my presentation, and Mike and Lucas keep not showing up. I'm almost worried something's wrong, like maybe they took a detour on the way and got lost. Maybe they're just bailing. But I don't believe that, I *can't* believe that. They said they'd be here.

The viewing period comes to an end, and everyone floods out of the expo hall to head to the ballroom for the awards ceremony. Eddie is silent by my side as I scan every face in the crowd, looking for my friends. All I see are dozens of students with circles of supporters around them, sharing embraces, talking about their projects, and beaming with pride. Even Anika's parents are here; they're looking severe and intense on either side of her, but they're *here*. The doors to the lobby entrance remain unmoving, no one arriving or leaving.

Dread sinks heavy in my stomach as the realization

spreads through me. I'm spinning with anger, hurt, betrayal, but none of it is bubbling up to the surface, just simmering underneath. It makes me feel small and pathetic. I can't even muster up a tantrum, which I feel like I deserve.

All I can do is nod, like this was the *only* outcome, like I should have expected it.

I probably should have.

Because my friends aren't coming.

# CHAPTER TWENTY-ONE

## SATURDAY, DECEMBER 7, 1985
## 4:03 P.M.

I'm sure Eddie notices my stormy mood, but there's no time to get into it before the awards ceremony. Danny, Eddie, and I shuffle into the hall together, where Anika is already sitting with her parents.

The clouds of my disappointment part briefly when Anika wins first place. Danny, Eddie, and I clap and cheer so raucously that even Anika's *parents* give us dirty looks as they applaud politely while Anika heads to the stage to accept the trophy.

Otherwise, the closing remarks pass in a blur, until suddenly, people are standing up and filing out of the auditorium.

And just like that, the science fair is over.

Danny, Eddie, and I trail out into the lobby where everyone is saying congratulation and goodbye and beginning to haul projects from the expo hall out into the world.

"Mr. Eddie!" someone calls. We stop, and the same girl from earlier is looking up at Eddie with wide eyes. "Is it true what you said about the curse?"

"There's no way," says a boy beside her. "The ancient wizard? The desecrated burial grounds? The crop circles? I'd believe one, but all three?"

Eddie smiles and I realize that this must have been how he delayed the start of the judging—more horror stories, presumably about the science fair curse. Which we've proven false today, but for the sake of dramatics, I'll let Eddie have this one.

"Oh, you naive little children," Eddie says, with a mischievous smile on his face. "Anything is possible, and here's why—"

Danny and I leave Eddie, who's launching into more stories, a small circle of students quickly gathering around him. At least Eddie had a decent time today, whether he cares about science or not.

We head into the expo hall to start collecting our projects. As Danny grabs Frodo's leash, I see Anika standing at her booth with her parents. Danny, Frodo, and I rush over to her.

"Holy shit, Anika!" I say. Her parents give me matching

disapproving glares that I barely register. "You're a genuine science celebrity now! How does it feel?"

Anika's eyes go wide and she gives an apologetic glance at her parents before stepping aside with me and Danny.

"Congrats, Anika," Danny says. "You deserve it, without a doubt."

"Thanks, you guys," she says. "I'm really glad I met all of you." She squats down and pats Frodo on the head. "Even you, Mr. Quackins."

I smile, because I feel the same, but my smile doesn't quite reach my eyes. It's hard to ignore the gaping lack of my friends. I'd wanted Mike and Lucas to meet Danny and Anika, to meet *Frodo,* to see the Bard Box in action, to be part of this, part of my life.

But they aren't. They just don't care enough.

"What's wrong with you, anyway, Mr. Frowny-Face?" Danny asks, nudging me with his elbow. "We solved the mystery, I thought you'd be excited."

"I am," I say, but the words come out with an air of defeat that betrays my mood.

I look at these new friends of mine, friends who have counted on me and trusted me all day to make the big calls and help bring the saboteur to justice, and it seems ridiculous that they've trusted me so much when I'm just . . . me. Dustin, the same loser who gets basketballs thrown at him in the cafeteria, the same loser whose friends can't bother to show up.

"I just . . . I don't know. I act all confident and put

together." I shrug, self-deprecating. "But the truth is, I'm just some loser who's here competing on my own because my only friends didn't want to do it with me. They didn't even want to come see me."

I wince, avoiding the group's eyes, waiting for the inevitable laughter and teasing.

"No offense, Dustin, but that's a load of hooey," says Danny. That surprises me so much my jaw drops as I turn to look at him. "I'm here with a project I did alone too."

"Me too," says Anika. "And the only people who showed up were my parents, because all they care about in my life is academia. Maybe it *does* make us losers, but we're not losers alone, at least."

Danny nods and beams like Anika took the words right out of his mouth.

I smile, and this time it feels more real.

"Up until today, Frodo was basically my only friend," Danny admits. "And he's a great listener, but he doesn't have much to say."

Frodo quacks as if in protest and then pecks at Danny's shoe, like he's chastising him. I can't help it—I burst out laughing. Anika holds it in for a beat longer, but then she's shaking with laughter, hand covering her mouth as she giggles.

And even if my friends ditched me, even if they couldn't bother to show up as a consolation when they didn't want to participate, at least there's this. Good people. New friends. A weirdly talented duck named Frodo Quackins.

And Eddie, who's still cornered in the lobby by a handful of students, presumably demanding more scary stories from him.

I wish Mike and Lucas cared enough to share in it with me. But for now, it's not too bad for a day's work.

▶

The drive home with Eddie is a lot calmer than our morning ride. Eddie has a tamer, spookier mixtape to play, Black Sabbath, Metallica, and some stuff I don't recognize. I'm quiet and contemplative, spending most of the drive with my arms crossed, looking out the window.

I'm trying not to feel too betrayed, but it's hard. I keep trying to make excuses for Mike and Lucas and why they might not have come, but I keep coming back to the fact that they *didn't*. They didn't even call. They just left me hanging. Which feels like a recurring theme over the last few months, and I don't love it.

Eddie swerves to a squealing stop in front of my house, having driven us back in record time by breaking every speed limit along the way. My street is quiet and dark, the streetlights illuminating us as we get out of the van. Eddie opens up the back so I can grab the Bard Box.

"Well, you basically sponsored this quest," I say, holding the Bard Box. "It's only appropriate you get your reward."

I extend the Bard Box to him in offering.

Eddie leans to one side to inspect it appraisingly. Then—

"Nah," he says.

My eyes narrow, my grip tightening on the Bard Box.

"What?" I ask. "That was the deal. You drive me, you get the Bard Box."

Eddie rolls his eyes like *I'm* the one being ridiculous.

"Come on, man, I was never gonna take your pride and joy," he says. "I would have been happy with a six-pack, honestly."

I don't point out once again that I'm fourteen and that beer wouldn't have been a reasonable request. But still, this is—not quite computing.

"You spent your whole day driving me to and from Indianapolis and babysitting a duck," I point out.

"That I did," Eddie says with a grimace, like he can't believe it himself. Then he shrugs. "I guess that's just what friends do for friends in need."

For some reason, that hits me like a punch to the gut, and I feel tears prickling behind my eyes, which is *mortifying* and *unacceptable*. I blink rapidly, nodding slowly in a way that I hope seems unbothered. I have a feeling Eddie sees right through it.

"Right," I say. "Thanks."

Eddie closes the back of the van, grins, and offers a little salute with two fingers.

"See you around, Henderson," he says.

He goes back to the driver's seat, hops in, and revs the engine. Soon enough, his van is skidding away.

I start to haul the Bard Box and my poster board inside,

but stop when I see the glow of the streetlights illuminating two bikes that lie in the driveway. I recognize them immediately as Mike's and Lucas's.

The sight should raise my spirits—they're here? They came? Maybe they *do* care? Maybe there *is* a reasonable explanation for them ditching me?—but instead, it fills me with dread. I'm just—exhausted, really, and I don't want to have to deal with whatever excuses they might offer. I kind of just want to fall into bed and sleep for a week.

I find Mike and Lucas at the kitchen table with a stack of rented movies. Lucas is in his basketball uniform. Something squeezes in my chest painfully at the sight.

I approach, and they both perk up, smiling, but casually, like they haven't stood me up on what should have been the best day of my life. I'm trying hard not to scowl, to be cool, but it's difficult.

"Hey! I hope it's okay, we let ourselves in with the key under the mat," says Lucas.

"How was the science fair?" Mike asks.

"It was fine," I say. As much as I'd wanted to tell them everything about the mystery and the saboteur earlier, now I just want to get rid of them.

Mike seems to pick up on my sour mood, which means I'm not doing half as well at playing it cool as I thought I was.

"Look," he says with a grimace, "Nancy's newspaper thing went long, so we couldn't get a ride. . . ."

"So I went to my basketball practice," Lucas says, "but

we wanted to at least congratulate you."

"You should have called the convention center," I say. "I was waiting around for you guys."

I don't say, *Everyone else had friends and family there. I don't say, I was counting on you. I don't say, I thought you cared a little more than that.*

Mike and Lucas exchange guilty looks. The part of me that's angry—a part that's growing rapidly—thinks, *Good.*

"That's why we wanted to be here when you got home," Lucas says.

"We brought some movies and thought we could order pizza or something," Mike offers.

I don't know why, but this is the thing that breaks me. This consolation prize for them not showing up, which was *already* a consolation prize for them not doing the fair with me in the first place. Disappointments on disappointments on disappointments. It feels like the confirmation of all of my fears since high school started—that my friends are changing too fast for me to change with them. That they don't care, and they're leaving me behind.

I can't hold back any longer. The quiet disappointment of the last few hours surges into anger and indignation.

"Do you guys think this makes up for you being crummy friends for, like, *months*?"

"Come on, man," Mike says. "What's that supposed to mean?"

I can't take it back now. I don't even want to.

"Exactly what I just said," I say, crossing my arms over

my chest. "You guys have been *terrible friends.*"

"I'm sorry?" Lucas says, not sounding sorry at all. "*We are* terrible for not coming to your science fair. But you being a total jerk about me joining the basketball team, *that's* not terrible, too?"

I roll my eyes. How can he even make that comparison?

"I have been giving you a completely reasonable amount of crap, considering how ridiculous it is," I say.

"That is exactly what I'm talking about!" Lucas says. "You won't take it seriously even though I've *told* you that it's important to me."

"Guys, please, can we—" Mike tries.

"Yeah, more important than your *friends,*" I say. "You've made that perfectly clear."

"And *you've* been a perfect friend?" Lucas asks.

"Yes, actually!" I burst out, nearly laughing at the question. I'm the *only* one who's cared about the party, who's tried to keep us together while everything has been falling apart.

Lucas stares me down and shakes his head like he can't believe what I'm saying. When he opens his mouth again, his voice is deadly serious, level and even.

"Max and I broke up, did you even know that?" he asks.

That stuns me right into silence. Because I *didn't* know. Why hadn't he told me? Why—

Why hadn't I asked?

"When?" I ask. Not *why,* because Max has been distant for long enough that that feels obvious.

"Thanksgiving," Lucas says. "While you've been busy playing with your experiments, the rest of us have been dealing with real life."

I feel frozen, like my blood has turned to ice in my veins, like I can't move except to slowly turn my head toward Mike.

"Did you know about it?" I ask.

Mike nods, looking very much like he doesn't want to be caught in the middle of this. Usually *I'm* the one mediating between Mike and Lucas, and I don't think *any* of us like that we've shuffled the arrangement.

"I . . . ," I start. But what do I even say to that? To the knowledge that I'm the last to know, that no one thought to clue me in. That they didn't care enough to tell me. That they didn't think *I'd* care enough to want to know. "I'm sorry to hear that. Seriously. But it's been a long day. Can we . . . do this on Monday? Can you guys just go home?"

"Dustin, come on—" Mike says.

"No, he's right," says Lucas. "We should go."

He gets up from the table and stalks out of the kitchen, while Mike lingers a moment longer.

I'm not sure if I should be protesting and apologizing or yelling at them more, and the uncertainty alone is proof that I need space and sleep before I talk to either of them again. But mostly, when Mike leaves too, I'm just relieved.

The front door creaks open and clicks closed behind them. Their muffled voices say *something* as they grab their bikes and ride off. But I'm not listening. I'm still standing in the kitchen, right where they left me, rooted to the spot. Alone, save for the Bard Box.

And Tews, who rubs up against my leg, reminding me it's her dinnertime. This finally breaks me out of my spell, because even though I've had the worst end to the day, I'm not going to punish Tews for that. I bend down to pet her, and something in my pocket pokes me.

I reach into the pocket and pull out a piece of thick paper. It's the business card Mr. Adams gave me in case I had questions about Eastwood. I thumb the embossed lettering.

I should throw it out.

I don't. I put it on the fridge with a magnet and then go to feed Tews.

And I do what I told Mr. Adams I'd do: I think about it.

# PART FOUR

# CHAPTER TWENTY-TWO

## SUNDAY, DECEMBER 8, 1985

"Suzie, do you copy? It's Dustin, come in."

It's not our usual day or time to call, so I'm not sure she'll be there. Sundays and Mondays are hardest to talk with Suzie—she's not supposed to use her radio or her computer since she's supposed to be focused on family and God, or whatever.

It takes a minute, but the radio crackles to life.

*"I hear you loud and clear, Dusty-bun!"*

I practically fall into my desk chair with a sigh, more grateful than ever after yesterday for the sound of her voice.

"Hey," I say. And my voice must sound as dejected as I feel, because Suzie's response is instant.

"What's wrong, Dusty-bun?" she asks. "Did something happen at the science fair?"

"God, I miss you," I sigh. "And I know you're not supposed to use the radio on Sundays, but—"

"I miss you too, Dusty," Suzie says. "Father is out right now, so I have a few minutes, but he'll be home soon."

"That's okay," I say. "I just wanted to hear your voice."

Suzie giggles, the sound filling my stomach with butterflies.

"Well, tell me what's got you down, then, Dusty," she says.

I'm just about to when—

"Suzie, get off the damn radio!" A voice that sounds like Suzie's older sister, Eden, bursts through the radio, accompanied by a slamming door.

"Get out of my room!" Suzie says.

"Suzie, I mean it. Father's going to have your head—"

The radio cuts out for a long minute, and I'm guessing Eden and Suzie are arguing. I wait it out. I'm used to Suzie's family hijinks at this point, but I'd be lying if I said I'm not especially disappointed right now. I could really use a good chat with Suzie, but it's looking like that will be difficult.

"I'm sorry, Dusty, I need to go. You'll give me the full update on Wednesday, right?" she asks, referring to our usual call time.

"Yeah," I say, stomach sinking, but I try to hide my disappointment. "I'll tell you everything then."

It just means I have to deal with the storm of thoughts in my head some other way.

▶

12/8/1985

Dear Will,

I hope you're doing well! I promised I'd write to you after the science fair. The title page you made looked perfect, so thank you again for that.

The science fair was . . . mostly really good.

The Bard Box was great, and I made friends, and I solved a yearslong case of academic sabotage. I tried new things! And it was awesome!

And the whole time, I couldn't wait to tell you guys about it all.

But then it turned out Mike and Lucas couldn't come. Which sucked.

We kind of had an argument when I got home. I was upset, and admittedly I may have been a bit of a jerk. And maybe I didn't explain myself well enough, that it wasn't <u>just</u> about the science fair but about months of them growing distant, of things <u>changing</u>.

But maybe that's the problem. Maybe I _need_ some change. Something that doesn't have anything to do with my friends, and has everything to do with _me_.

Yesterday, I was approached about . . . let's call it a new solo quest. It promises adventure, and treasure, and experience points. And it's _definitely_ a big change. It could be good. Maybe.

But I feel like a traitor for even considering it. The party means everything to me. You know that.

~~I just don't know if it means anything to them anymore.~~

Anyway. You wanted to know about the fair, so I'll stick to the fun parts. The academic wonderland. The mystery at play. The new friends. This is about to be a long story—and you will _love_ the quirky animal companion. . . .

▶

I emerge from my room and come downstairs far later than my mother ever allows, even on weekends. I head to the kitchen, ready to brave the day, determined to try to be a person despite feeling like a zombie.

Two things quickly become apparent.

First, Mike and Lucas accidentally left their stack of movies when fleeing last night.

Second, I blew the money my mom gave me for takeout on road trip snacks, so all I have to eat is assorted junk food, unless I want to cook, which I don't.

All this to say, I have no choice but to spend my Sunday eating my feelings on the couch, watching movies alone that I should have been watching with my so-called best friends. Movies and snacks—at least *they* are consistent and reliable.

I'm halfway through *Tron,* but to be honest, I haven't processed any of it. I'm zoned out, thinking about my fight with Lucas and Mike and pondering that offer from Mr. Adams. All these emotions I can't identify swirl around my head like Saturn's rings, a million particles, small and large, representing a million thoughts, in endless orbit.

My best friends, disappointing me over and over again. I'm sick of always being the one who cares the most.

A spot at Eastwood, if I wanted. A scholarship, if I needed. Where I could explore science and technology with the best and brightest, and with real support.

My best friends, growing up, growing apart. Whatever you want to call it, the key factor is they're leaving me behind.

A spot at Eastwood, where I have the chance to start over, to follow my dreams, to do something for myself.

My *best friends,* breaking up without feeling like they needed to tell me. My best friends, not feeling like they *could* tell me. My best friends—the looks on Mike's and Lucas's faces when I told them to leave.

The front door opens with a squeak that pulls me from my thoughts, and then my mom is walking through the door with her rolling suitcase behind her.

"Dusty!" She beams, leaving her bag at the door and coming over to the couch to pinch my cheeks, which she *knows* I hate and which I allow only because I'm beyond relieved to see her. "How was the science fair?"

The brief relief is replaced with dread again.

"Uh, it was good," I say noncommittally. "How was your trip? And Aunt Kathy's birthday?"

"It was fun, all lovely! You know how Aunt Kathy is, nonstop chatter and a little bit too much white wine, but—" She cuts off with a gasp when Tews rubs up against her legs. "Oh, Tews! Hi, darling!" She scoops the cat up and showers her with kisses. "But tell me more about the fair! I was sure you'd call last night to tell me all about it. Did you forget Aunt Kathy's number? I wrote it down for you, didn't I?"

"No, I know it," I say. "I just had a long day, I guess."

"But it was good? Your project went okay? Your friends came?"

She's so enthusiastic, and interested, and *clueless* about everything that went down that I feel on the verge of laughter and tears all at once. It completely robs me of any hopes of playing things off like they're fine.

And I break again, burying my face in my hands, words

spilling into my palms in a muffled jumble: "My friends ditched me, and it's maybe my fault for being an asshole, and now I have to run away to a boarding school in Ohio."

"What?" Mom asks.

"Nothing," I say. "Everything sucks."

I feel my mom's hand on my back and Tews crawling into my lap. "Just slow it down for me, baby."

I stop hiding behind my hands and take a deep breath, distracting myself by petting Tews's silky fur. "I'm fine, really," I say. "I have snacks, so I'm great."

The coffee table is littered with wrappers as evidence.

My mom puts her hand on her hips and looks at me sternly. "How many Little Debbies have you eaten?"

"A normal amount," I lie, plucking up the empty wrappers to hide them.

"Have you eaten *anything* but junk all day?"

I haven't eaten anything but junk all *weekend*.

"No," I admit.

My mom sighs. "I'm making soup."

"You don't have to do that," I say. But I'd be lying if I said I wasn't in dire need of a vegetable or two.

"I'm making soup," Mom says again, determined.

I almost protest more, but she is already marching into the kitchen. I emerge from my cocoon on the couch and find her already flinging open cabinets and gathering ingredients.

"Now, do you want to tell me about the science fair, from the beginning?" she asks.

I don't know where to begin, and as I'm hunting for where to start, my mom goes to the fridge to get food.

Except, she's stopped with the door closed, looking at something in her hand. It takes me a moment to realize that she's holding the Eastwood Academy business card, which I'd left on the fridge.

"Who's this from?" my mom asks. Not accusatory, just curious.

"Oh, yeah," I say, as if I'd forgotten all about it. "I . . . I mean, it's probably nothing."

Either that, or it's the ticket to an entire new future I didn't know I wanted. Who's to say?

"Eastwood Academy," she says. "This is that fancy science boarding school in Ohio, isn't it?" I'm surprised she knows about it, but then, she's always been the one researching science camps and such for me to attend, so I guess it makes sense that it's on her radar.

"Uh, yeah. There was this guy at the science fair who I guess was impressed with me?" I say, rubbing the back of my neck. "He wanted me to consider applying. Said something about scholarships. I don't know, it's not a big deal."

I don't know why I feel the need to minimize it. Like, if I acknowledge how exciting it is, it's like admitting that I'm considering it. That I *want* it. And that feels like a betrayal of the highest order.

"That's amazing, baby! This is a *huge* deal!" my mom exclaims. She hugs me, squeezing so tightly that I can't breathe until she pulls back, placing her hands on my shoulders, her eyes wide. "Schools like Eastwood can give you a huge leg up for colleges, and careers, and *life*—"

"But I *can't,* right?" I say. "I mean, *you're* here, and my friends are here. . . ."

My mom's brows draw together as she gives me a confused smile.

"Dusty, this is a huge opportunity," she says. "Your friends would understand. And I somehow survived decades on my own before you came into my life, so I think *I'd* be okay. I'd miss you of course. I mean, *boarding school,* wow. But you can't make this decision based on me, or on your friends. You have to make it for yourself."

Maybe it's just that I had been so quick to dismiss the idea immediately, but I can't believe how enthusiastic she is right off the bat, how *seriously* she's taking it. Like it's really an option.

I swallow hard, and my voice is small when I speak. "You really think . . ." I clear my throat. "I mean, you don't think the idea is ridiculous? You think I should consider it?"

"Of course, sweetheart," she says. "There's nothing ridiculous about that big, talented brain of yours. Is this why you fought with your friends? They don't want you to leave?"

I almost laugh. The problem is that I don't know if they'll even *care* if I leave.

I haven't told my mom about the fight with Lucas and

Mike. But she's so proud of me, so smiley, that I don't want to break it to her. More than that, I don't want to have to admit that I'm at fault too.

"Something like that," I say.

But she's right about one thing: this could be a big opportunity. I can't just dismiss it. Will and El leaving felt so tragic in some ways, but this isn't the same. This isn't running from monsters and international conspiracies, it's running *to* something, a chance to be somewhere better. And maybe Will and El struggled in a new place, but they're doing well *now*. At least, that's how it seems from the letters. Maybe a big change like that really can be a good thing.

"I'll call tomorrow. Just to ask some questions and find out what the application process would look like. I'm not committing to anything, but I'll . . . hear him out."

"That sounds like a good plan," Mom says. "Do you want me to be there for the call? Or help you come up with questions to ask?"

"I think I've got it," I say. "But thank you."

I should say that to my mom more often, really.

She hugs me, kisses the top of my head, and goes back to making soup.

▶

After my mom has force-fed me a gallon of vegetable soup, I gather up the videos Mike and Lucas left behind and ride my bike over to Family Video despite the December cold.

It's just Steve tonight, and he's flipping the sign on the window to Closed as I burst through the entrance. He stumbles back so the door doesn't hit him in the face.

"Watch it, dude, what the hell?" he says, closing the door behind me as I storm inside. "We're closing in two minutes, what are you doing here?"

"I need to talk to you," I say. "It's urgent."

"Urgent as in life or death?" he asks, skeptical. "Or high school drama?"

"Potentially both," I say.

Steve rolls his eyes and lets out a put-upon sigh, then defeatedly gestures toward the counter and its stool in invitation.

"Step into my office, then," he says.

He locks the door so no customers can come in, and I collapse onto the stool.

"What's wrong?" Steve asks. "Wasn't the science fair yesterday? I thought you'd be all jazzed—"

"I need to ask your opinion on something, but you have to swear not to tell another soul," I say.

"Sure, okay, whatever," he says, another eye roll punctuating that he's not taking this seriously.

"I mean it, Steve, this goes to your *grave*," I insist.

"Okay! God! I won't say a word, I swear," he says. "A little trust, Henderson?"

"I know," I say.

Of course I trust him. That's why I'm here, because

I need his opinion just as badly as I needed my mother's opinion.

Steve leans on the counter, all ears despite his whining.

I tell him everything.

I tell him about solving the mystery at the science fair and catching Brian, and about making new friends in Danny and Anika. I tell him about Eddie being the only one who was there for me all day, while my friends ditched me. I tell him about Mike and Lucas waiting at my house when I got home and how I blew up at them, how Lucas probably hates me, and how it all seems to be my fault.

And finally, I tell him about the scholarship offer to the fancy science school, and how I'm considering it a lot more seriously than I would have ever thought I would.

He listens to it all carefully, quietly, lets me ramble and talk fast as it all rushes out.

"Wow," Steve says, once my words finally slow to a stop. "That's . . . wow."

"Yeah," I say.

He scratches the back of his head, considering the avalanche of information I've dropped on him.

"I mean, dude, this is impressive, and you deserve it," he says. "But you'd really leave Hawkins? Leave your friends?"

And I get his concern. Because the party barely survived Will and El leaving, and if I go, the house of cards could really, finally, and completely collapse. But—

"If we're growing apart anyway, maybe it'd be for the best," I say.

It's the cold truth that I don't want to admit but that is hard to argue against.

"You don't really believe that," Steve says immediately, with the kind of scolding tone my mom uses when I accidentally let out a curse word in front of her. "They've been your friends since you were in diapers—"

"Fourth grade," I correct.

"Yeah, *infancy* basically—and you're going to let this come between you?" he asks, shaking his head in disbelief. "No way. You said yourself you're aware you've been an asshole, right? You've *all* been assholes. So at least *try* to talk to them. Give them a chance to apologize. And for that matter, maybe apologize to them too?"

"It's not that easy," I say.

"It actually really is."

"It really isn't."

"It *really is* and we are *not* doing this back-and-forth thing all day so let's leave it there."

*"Fine,"* I grit out.

*"Good,"* says Steve, giving me his signature stern-mom look. Then he softens a little and adds, "Are you going to apologize?"

"I don't know!" I say, miserable. "I came over here so you could make me feel better, not nag me."

"I can do both," he says. "Especially when the reason you're feeling bad is totally solvable."

I refrain from telling him that it doesn't feel that way, lest we end up bickering again.

"But what about Eastwood?" I ask.

"Do you actually want to go there?" Steve asks. "Like, yeah, it's a great opportunity, but do you actually *want* it? Or are you just trying to run away from the fact that your friends are being jerks or whatever?"

I scowl, crossing my arms in front of my chest, a bit defensive. "It can be both," I say.

Steve sighs. "Dude, just . . . talk to your friends, okay?" he pleads. "Don't make a decision based on how you're feeling without even trying to fix it."

I scowl, mostly because I know he's right.

"I'm calling Mr. Adams tomorrow," I say. "Just to get more information. But . . . I'll talk to Mike too."

"And Lucas," Steve corrects.

I hate it when he's right.

"I'll *try*," I say, "to figure out *how* to approach Lucas without making us both into bigger assholes. Okay? Happy?"

"Thrilled," Steve deadpans. Then he frowns and adds, "I'm glad you came to me, though. I know you've been worshiping your new best friend Eddie recently, and . . . Whatever. Now, do you need a ride home? It's getting dark."

He changes the subject so quickly I barely have time to process that Steve, normally so self-assured, might actually have been worried I liked Eddie more than him, or something. Robin had made jokes, but I always thought that was all they were. It's ridiculous—Steve is and will always be one of my best friends. He seems eager to move past the topic of Eddie, so I let it go.

"Maybe," I say. "But first . . ." I brighten up a little, nodding to a poster behind him. "Didn't Gremlins just come out on VHS?"

Steve rolls his eyes like it's some great inconvenience, but I know he doesn't really mind.

"It sure did, dude, hold on." He sighs, and turns to dig through the new releases.

My stomach twists in nervous anticipation. Because tomorrow, I'm going to talk to my friends, and I'm going to consider the possibility of a future at Eastwood. And things might be changing, they might be more different than ever, but I know that in the end, everything is going to be okay.

# CHAPTER TWENTY-THREE

## MONDAY, DECEMBER 9, 1985

I don't know what to expect when I go to school on Monday, whether I should be avoiding my friends or if *they'll* be avoiding *me*. Or if maybe we're all going to pretend everything's fine and go about our days like normal. But I promised Steve I would at least *try* to talk to them, so I go out of my way to find Mike before the first bell rings.

He's rifling through his locker for a textbook, and I rap my fist twice on the locker's open door to alert him of my presence, like he's an animal I don't want to spook.

Mike looks up and tries to hide his surprise, but fails. His eyebrows raise and then lower as a dozen different reactions flicker across his face—surprise, concern, hurt—

before he presses his lips together in a firm line.

"Hey," he says, his face having settled into a neutral expression.

"Hey," I say.

I don't know where to start. I haven't been as much of a jerk to Mike as I have to Lucas, but I've been upset with *both* of them, so I really don't know where we stand.

"Look, I know you've been an asshole, and I know I've been an asshole, but I refuse to stoop to the immaturity of silent treatment. I just want us to be okay. So . . . are we? Okay?"

Mike tilts his head, considering this. I almost can't breathe with the anticipation, but he finally lets out a sigh.

"Yeah, we're cool," he says, then gives me an apologetic grimace. "It's really Lucas you've gotta talk to."

Don't I know it. "Yeah," I say, "but I was a jerk to you too. . . ." It feels like I'm getting let off too easy.

"Yeah, but so was I." Mike shakes his head with a self-deprecating laugh. "Look, I'm sorry. Seriously. I've been distant, I know."

I inhale a sharp breath. I've felt Mike's distance, but I never thought he'd apologize for it. I didn't think he even realized.

"I've been worried about El," he says, voice quiet. I think it might be the most honest he's been with me in a while. "I've been so focused on missing her, and Will, and I guess I kind of . . . forgot about the best friends I still have here with me."

My heart squeezes, because I know what he means all too well. I've been so focused on what the party used to be that I haven't focused on what it could be, what it *is*.

"I'm sure it didn't help that I was being a self-absorbed asshole," I say. It's not quite an apology, but I hope he understands that it's implied.

"You weren't, dude, really," Mike says. "For what it's worth, I'd really like to hear about the science fair, if you still want to share."

Relief washes over me like a tide, and I relax, sagging like an invisible weight has been lifted from my shoulders as muscles I didn't even know were clenched begin to relax.

"Thanks, Mike," I say. "And you can talk to me too. About El, and Will? I miss them too, you know."

Mike blinks a few times, his mouth twisting up, and he's about to say something, but he's interrupted by—

*WHAM!*

A basketball crashes into his locker, missing my face by mere inches and almost slamming the locker door closed on Mike's fingers.

There's scattered laughter behind us, and a very unapologetic *"My bad,"* as Jason Carver picks up the ball, snickering to himself.

Annoyance prickles my skin. I bite my cheek to keep from telling the guy to shove it, because picking fights will not do me any good. But this is the perfect reminder of why Eastwood calls to me so much. Surely Eastwood doesn't have letterman-jacket-clad bullies, doesn't have basketballs thrown viciously in cafeterias and hallways, doesn't have meatheads laughing about it all.

I'm glaring at the sea of green letterman jackets passing us when I see Lucas. He's watching me and Mike closely.

Then—

"We should try to be careful in the halls," Lucas says, voice careful, but I know him well enough to hear the slight waver. "So we don't hit anyone."

It's so small an interjection. Barely a defense at all. But it's *something.*

"Yeah, whatever, Sinclair," laughs Jason and his cronies, unbothered.

The herd of jocks continues to move down the hall, and Lucas hesitates a beat. He gives me a tiny, wavering not-quite smile. Then he follows the group.

As soon as they're gone, Mike smacks my shoulder.

"Dude, that was your chance," he says. "He's trying, you know?"

I'm so pleasantly surprised by the interaction that I have to shake myself out of my amazement to return my attention to Mike.

"Yeah, I know," I say. Then, determined, "I'm going to try, too."

Because Lucas doesn't completely hate me.

And I could never hate him.

I need to fix things. Even if I'm still considering the Eastwood offer, when just thinking about it makes me feel guilty.

The bell rings, and Mike and I go our separate ways to homeroom.

I had promised Steve I would talk to my friends, and I'd also promised my mom I would call Mr. Adams.

And I owe it to myself to do both.

▶

I call Mr. Adams from school during free period because I'm too antsy to wait until I get home. Students flurry around me, chatting and heading toward different classes and activities, while I duck toward the pay phone.

I dial the number, the business card slightly crumpled because I've been nervously fiddling with its edges the past few days. I stare at the phone and the hastily scribbled graffiti, eyes unfocused, as the phone rings in my ears, and I try to steel my nerves.

*Click.* The call connects. An inhale of breath. And—

*"Dennis Adams speaking."*

"Hi," I say, and my brain for some reason gets stuck on *Dennis.* I swallow hard and shake my head quickly as if that will dislodge the thought and clear the way for something that makes sense. "It's Dustin? Henderson? From the science fair?"

*"Yes, I remember, of course!"* Mr. Adams says, and I can hear him perk up through the phone. *"It's good to hear from you. All is well, I hope?"*

"Uh, yeah," I say, which is maybe a lie, but Mr. Adams

doesn't need to know the details of my inner turmoil. "I think I'm interested in Eastwood. Maybe. I was wondering if we could talk more about it—as a completely theoretical possibility."

*"That's excellent to hear! Even if purely theoretical,"* he says. Over the line, a school bell rings shrilly. *"Look, I have a meeting in just a few minutes, but how about we set up a time, and I'll have another person from the admissions board here, and we can talk more extensively? It's not an interview, nothing so formal. It's really just a chance for us to get to know you and for you to ask some questions."*

"That kind of sounds like an interview," I point out before I can bite my tongue.

Luckily, Mr. Adams just laughs.

*"Yes, I suppose it does. How does end of day on Friday work for you? Maybe five-thirty? You can call me at this number."*

I have Hellfire Club on Friday, but I should still have enough time to get home and make the call.

"That would be great," I say. "Thank you."

*"Of course. I'll speak to you then,"* Mr. Adams says. *"And, Dustin?"*

"Yeah?"

*"I'm really glad you called. I think you'd do well at Eastwood, truly."*

"Yeah," I say. The fact that I agree wholeheartedly makes my stomach hurt. "I'll talk to you Friday, then."

# CHAPTER
# TWENTY-FOUR

## TUESDAY, DECEMBER 10, 1985

The next day, I go to the gym for my free period and find the basketball team having a practice game among themselves. I linger in the doorway, out of sight, and watch.

I've never loved sports. I understand the appeal of games, of course, in the strategic sense, but throwing balls through baskets or running them past lines on a field isn't satisfying to me the way that real problem-solving is. It doesn't help that I've always associated sports with the jocks who play them who knock me and the other nerds of the world around for fun.

But now, watching Lucas sprinting, dribbling the ball, shouting something to a teammate, and taking a shot, I kind of get it. It's exciting in its own way, just like a tense D&D fight can be. There's push and pull, stakes and passion, like a good story. Lucas shoots, and the basketball circles the rim for a second before sinking into the basket. A couple of the guys on Lucas's team thump him on the back, and he smiles to himself, pleased.

I can't help it. I bring my hands together, applauding enthusiastically, cheering for my friend. And effectively drawing the attention of everyone in the gym.

"Let's take five, guys," barks the coach, jotting something on a clipboard and then joining a circle of players to talk.

Lucas jogs over to me, wiping sweat from his forehead with the back of his hand. I can tell he's hesitant from the way he comes to a slow stop and continues to shuffle his feet in place. Like he's ready to turn heel and flee if this conversation goes wrong.

I really hope it doesn't go wrong.

I'm nervous too, to be fair, palms sweating, tugging at the ends of my sleeves, because I want so badly for everything to be okay. I suddenly wonder if he's just coming over here to tell me to get lost. I'll be lucky if he even hears me out. Still, I aim for casual, even as nerves flare in my chest and stomach.

"You know, I don't even really know the rules of basketball?" I say. "Like, besides the goal of getting the ball in the basket."

"There's definitely more to it than that," Lucas says, carefully. He's got his guard up, and I can't blame him.

"Yeah, I'm getting that," I say. "Maybe I should learn. You know, if I want to understand what's going on if I come to one of your games."

Lucas studies me, his head tilted to one side. "You'd actually come to one of my games?"

"I mean, if you'd want me there," I say, wanting to give him an out, "considering how much of a dick I've been about it."

"You *have* been a dick," Lucas admits. "But obviously I'd want you there, dude."

"I mean, I still don't really get it?" I say. "But if it's what you want to do . . . I should have had your back. I'm sorry."

"You weren't totally wrong, though," Lucas says. "I was letting some of these jerks rub off on me and—that's not who I want to be."

He looks toward the court, where a few guys are chatting and laughing as they bounce a ball back and forth.

"I just . . . this is the first time I've had someone like *me* to look up to," Lucas says. "And I just wanted to impress him, and be like him, and—fit in. With him, and yeah, *all* the popular guys. But that doesn't matter. Even if I want to make new friends, I don't want you to think I'm leaving you guys behind. *Ever.* So, I'm sorry too."

And really, that's all I've wanted to hear from him all damn year. That we're still friends. That he's not trying to ditch us. That he still cares about our friendship, about the party. I'm so relieved I could cry.

"I don't know who drew first blood at this point," I

admit. "But . . ." I shove out my hand in offering. A truce.

Lucas's eyes go wide. A beat passes before he finally extends his hand to shake mine.

"Actually," he says, a bit shyly, "I thought, maybe, if it's not too late, I could still join Hellfire? If not for this campaign, then next semester's?"

I perk up immediately, my eyes widening, a smile spreading across my face.

"That can definitely be arranged," I say. Eddie's kind of intense about changes to the campaign, but I'm sure I can convince him to squeeze a new character into the final battles. "I'll talk to Eddie." An idea occurs to me, as if a lightbulb appears over my head, and I brighten. "On one condition."

"What?" Lucas asks.

"You have to explain the rules of basketball to me," I say. "So that when I'm on the bleachers watching your first game of the season, I can at least *kind of* know what's going on."

Lucas breaks into a grin, and I realize I haven't seen him smile in what feels like ages. It's nice to see it again.

"Yeah," Lucas says. "Yeah, I can do that."

And just like that, it feels like all is well again.

Or at least like everything will be, eventually.

▶

With a little bit of time left in my free period, I find Eddie in the AV room scribbling notes in his DM binder. I ask about Lucas joining us this week at Hellfire Club in a rushed flood of words.

Eddie narrows his eyes and closes the binder carefully, then folds his hands on top of it.

"Let me get this straight," he says. "You want me—in our last two sessions of the semester, and of the whole campaign—to add a brand-new character with a brand-new player to the mix? Instead of just waiting until we start a new campaign next semester?"

"Yep," I say. "That's basically it."

Eddie takes a deep breath like he's trying to calm himself. He taps the binder.

"Do you know what this is, Henderson?" he asks.

"Your Dungeon Master notes?" I answer, like it might be a trick question.

"My Dungeon Master notes," Eddie agrees. "Where I painstakingly plan out every detail and every possibility of every decision you and the other players could possibly make, and all of the ripples of repercussions of those decisions, so that I can run a game that is dynamic and, frankly, badass."

I gulp, because I can see where this is going. "Yeah," I squeak. "That's why you're such a great DM."

"I appreciate the flattery," Eddie deadpans. "But a new character this late in the game is not in the cards. And a new *player*? Out of the question. He can join next semester."

My heart sinks into my stomach, but I refuse to give up. It only makes me more determined.

"Eddie, Lucas is one of the best D&D players I've ever had the privilege of fighting alongside," I say. "We're not just adding him for fun. We *need* him. Really, between him and the rest of the Hellfire Club, there are no people I'd rather fight monsters with. Give him a chance. Please."

Eddie taps his fingers on the binder, considering, and then looks up at me through suspicious, narrowed eyes.

"Okay, hold on," he says. "Be honest. Is this really about D&D?"

"Yes!" I say, a little too loudly. Eddie's eyebrows arch even further, making it clear he does *not* believe me. I sigh, and admit, "But it's also that—we just made up, and we're on thin ice, and I just want to make sure I'm not leaving things on bad terms if I—"

I cut myself short. *If I'm leaving Hawkins for Eastwood.* Just the thought racks me with guilt, but there's also a thrill of excitement and anticipation that it's even a possibility.

Eddie raises an eyebrow and leans forward. "If you what, Henderson?"

My mouth twists as I debate whether I should tell him.

I've already told Steve, and my mom, but I don't want my friends to find out until and unless I'm certain I'm leaving. Mostly because I don't want them to try to talk me out of it.

But I trust Eddie. If this science fair has done anything, it's proved that he's on my side. I take the seat opposite him.

"Look, you can't tell anyone about this," I warn, voice low.

"Okay," he says easily.

"Seriously, Eddie, or I'll tell everyone how you screamed like a girl when you first saw Frodo Quackins."

"Dude, you don't need to blackmail me, I already said okay."

"Sorry," I say, sheepish. "I . . . I have this interview tomorrow. For the fancy science school from the fair? Eastwood? And I just . . . If I do it, I don't want it to be because I'm running away, and I don't want to leave things with my friends in a bad way."

Eddie reclines in his seat to regard me, impressed. "Damn. You're a busy dude, aren't you?"

I can't help but smile. "I swear I don't go looking for trouble, it just *finds* me."

"Bull," says Eddie. "You look for it."

I laugh and raise my hands in surrender, called out. "Okay, sometimes," I admit.

Eddie taps his chin thoughtfully. "I mean, obviously you'd do great at a science school," he says. "You don't need me to tell you that."

"Thanks," I say.

Eddie studies me a moment longer, then lets out a sigh, rolling his eyes so aggressively and theatrically that his head rolls back too.

*"Fine,"* he says. "If it's important to you—tell Sinclair to get me a character sheet by end of day *tomorrow,* okay? And I'll figure out a way to add him."

I leap up so enthusiastically I jolt the table.

"Thank you, thank you, thank you!"

Eddie rolls his eyes again, but it seems like it's just for show, if you ask me.

"This is a one-time thing," he insists. "If you *ever* ask me to alter a campaign's *finale* for you *again,* I will laugh in your face. Understood?"

"Understood," I agree.

And I'm so excited and relieved that I follow a whim and go around the table and hug Eddie around his shoulders. He pats my back awkwardly, not quite hugging me back, but it's close enough that I'll call it a win.

"Thank you!" I say again as I pull away. "I'll tell Lucas. We'll get it to you tomorrow, for sure."

I'm shouldering my backpack and preparing to bolt out of the room with newfound purpose, but just as my hand finds the doorknob Eddie calls out.

"Can I give you a word of advice?" he says. I pause and turn around to face him where he's sitting at the head of the table. "You can feel free to ignore it."

I nod for him to go on, giving him my rapt attention, my feet bringing me closer to the table.

"If this school is your dream, or whatever, you need to chase it," Eddie says. My chest tightens, my heart skipping a beat. "I mean, you clearly love science."

"Yeah," I say. "I do."

"And that's awesome. It's just . . ." Eddie fiddles with the rings on his fingers, which I recognize now as a nervous gesture. "Remember how competitive Brian was? And how intense Anika was? I guess I just worry that you'd go there and science wouldn't feel fun the way it does for you now. Things could be really different there, you know?"

And yeah, I know that. That's the *point*.

"Maybe I could use a little *different*," I say. "Maybe I *need* to change."

Eddie scoffs. "Bullshit."

I flinch at his lack of hesitation. "What's bullshit?"

"You don't need to change," Eddie says, like it's obvious. "You just gotta—keep doing your thing. That's why Eastwood wants you there. That's why your friends adore you, even when they're being little tools about it. That's why you're a hell of a player, and why I'd be bummed to lose you from the party in Hellfire."

I inhale sharply, breath puffing out my chest with surprised confidence at the compliments. Because Eddie is probably the coolest person I know, and compliments like those feel more valuable than a mint-condition first issue of *X-Men,* coming from him.

"But you shouldn't worry about that, about me, or your friends," he continues. "You need to worry about what *you* want to do. And don't do it for the sake of *changing.* Since I've met you, Henderson, you haven't let anyone tell you who to be. That's a good goddamn skill to have in this life. Don't lose that."

My breath catches, and I swallow hard around a newly forming lump in my throat. I'm simultaneously pleased at the praise and completely taken off guard by it. I've been worried about my friends changing, about me not changing with them, but maybe changing myself isn't the answer. Maybe when things are changing around us, the bravest thing we can do is be ourselves, no matter what everyone else is doing.

"Yeah," I say, and my voice comes out weak. "Yeah, I hear you."

"Good," says Eddie. "Now get out of here before I think too hard about how the hell I'm gonna add this new character, and change my mind."

"Right," I say, and head back to the door. I push it open, but before heading into the hallway, I pause and turn around once more. "And, Eddie?"

"Hmm?" Eddie hums, waiting for me to speak.

I have a lot of things swirling in my head, and a lot of things I want to say. I don't know where to start, but I'll keep it simple, for now.

"Thank you," I say.

Eddie smiles and tips an imaginary hat. "Anytime, kid."

# CHAPTER
# TWENTY-FIVE

## FRIDAY, DECEMBER 13, 1985

On the day of my Eastwood interview, and the day that
Lucas is supposed to finally join us for Hellfire Club, I wear
my Weird Al shirt.

I don't think it's what Eddie meant, exactly, when
he said to be myself, but it feels symbolic, appropriately
symmetrical, as I approach the end of my first semester of
high school.

Instead of heading straight into the school after I get
off the bus, I go around to the back of the building where
some students take smoke breaks. I'm relieved to see what
I'm looking for: red hair, a small frame, a skateboard.

I hang back a moment and watch as Max does a kick

flip, a maneuver I know she's been practicing for ages. She nails it.

"*Gnarly, dude!*" I call in an exaggeratedly terrible California-surfer-guy voice. Her head whips around. "That was, like, *totally tubular.*"

Max steps down on her skateboard to stop it from rolling away as she turns toward me.

"I think those words are more for surfing than skating," she says.

"Yeah, well, I don't know any skater-specific lingo."

Amusement tugs at Max's lips, but it's like she can't be persuaded to give a real smile. "That's probably for the best, considering how you misuse the slang you do know."

I laugh lightly, and dare to take a few steps closer. Max is like a startled animal, jolting at the movement, watching me warily like she's preparing to bolt.

"Max," I say. "We're still friends, aren't we?"

She blinks at me with owlishly wide eyes.

"Uh, I mean, yeah," she says. Then looks over her shoulder like I might be talking to someone hiding behind her. There is no one else. "Right?"

"Duh," I say, rolling my eyes. It's never been a question on my end. "I just—haven't seen much of you."

"Yeah, I guess I've been busy," she says dismissively, avoiding my gaze.

Her eyes flit around like she's looking for an escape. Which means I need to stop beating around the bush and say what I came here to say.

"I want you to know that we're here for you," I say, careful to annunciate the words so there's no chance of her misunderstanding. "The whole party is."

Max scoffs at the sincerity. "What is this? Are you dying?"

"Nope," I say. "Not dying. I'm trying to be a better friend."

"Okay, weirdo, sure," Max snorts, but her eyes soften like maybe she's just a *little* bit touched by it.

And that's good enough for me.

"You wouldn't want to play D&D with us tonight, would you?" I ask.

Max rolls her eyes. I've asked her enough times to know what the answer will be.

"Nope," she says, popping the *p*.

"Yeah, figured. Eddie would have killed me if I added another person, anyway," I admit. "I'll see you around though, okay? Don't be a stranger."

Max swallows hard, blinks quickly a few times like there's something in her eyes.

"Yeah, okay," she says. "I'll see you around."

She turns back to her skateboard, kicks off, and rolls away. I still wish I could do more, like make her stay and play D&D with us, but I let her go.

I said my piece: we're here for her. I don't know what she's going through, or what she needs, what kind of side quest she might be on.

But I hope that's enough.

▶

It is exactly one minute past the start time for Hellfire Club, and Lucas isn't here yet.

The table is full, save for a single chair next to mine. Eddie is shuffling through his DM binder, and Mike, Gareth, Jeff, and Doug are gathered with character sheets and dice sets laid out on the table. Me, I'm just staring at the minute hand of the clock as it *tick, tick, ticks* like it's trying to taunt me.

"Are we sure this new guy is coming?" Gareth asks, idly stacking his array of dice into a lopsided tower that topples over with a clatter.

"He's coming," I insist.

Because he said he would. And maybe that didn't mean anything when it came to the science fair, but I have to believe he means it this time.

The clock ticks its way to 3:02 just as the door to the AV room swings open, and Lucas enters the room.

"Hey, guys," he says. "Sorry—am I late?"

"Yes," Gareth grumbles.

At the same time, I say, "No, it's fine!" with more enthusiasm than necessary.

Because he came. Lucas is joining the Hellfire Club.

Lucas gives a sheepish smile as he slides off his backpack and sits in the last open chair, digging out his character sheet and a pencil.

"Thanks for joining us, Sinclair," Eddie says. "Let's get started, shall we?"

I'm almost nervous, in a way that I haven't been about

D&D since that time Mike and I almost died in Castle Ravenloft a few years ago. We haven't all played together in ages, and things have been so tense between us. What if it's not how it used to be?

But as Eddie launches into his theatrical narration, immersing us in the story, the nerves slowly crumble into nothing. Eddie introduces Lucas's character in such a natural way, and Lucas uses this awesome character voice that immediately impresses Gareth, Doug, and Jeff, and then—

We all get into it, which is easy to do when Eddie runs such amazing campaigns, and it helps that Lucas, Mike, and I know how to play off each other and work together, both in the role-playing parts and in battle. It's easy. It's *fun*. And it feels like this is how it's supposed to be. It might not be the whole party, and it might not be the same as it used to be, but it feels like the next best thing. Just playing my favorite game with some of my favorite people.

We're so engrossed that it feels like barely any time has passed before Eddie is wrapping up the session and telling us we'll finish the campaign next week and that we should be prepared to stay late if necessary.

Emerging from a really good session of D&D is kind of like leaving the movie theater in the daytime, when you've just spent two hours in a dark room and been transported to another world. Then, suddenly, you're faced with reality, and the bright glare of the sun, and it takes a minute to come back to yourself, to remember who and when and where you are.

So I blink away the haze of fantasy and magic in my mind to focus on the reality of our figurines on the battle map just as everyone's beginning to clean up, with Eddie gathering up the board pieces while we tuck away our character sheets.

"I'll be honest, Sinclair, I had doubts about adding someone so late," Eddie says. "But you were pretty damn awesome."

"I haven't played in what feels like forever," Lucas says, smiling and enthusiastic. "That was great. Thank you for letting me join so late, seriously."

"I'd say anytime," Eddie says, "but hopefully you'll join *on time* next semester."

"Definitely," says Lucas. "I'm in, totally. Sign me up."

"Seriously?" I ask, so enthused by *his* enthusiasm that the word comes out louder than intended.

"Yeah, seriously," Lucas says. "I want to do basketball *and* Hellfire. I never meant to just do one or the other. Everything has just been overwhelming and—I'm sorry it took me so long to come."

I'm grinning so wide that I probably look insane, so I duck my head to focus on packing up my stuff and putting on my jacket.

We all say our goodbyes and *see you next week*s and head out, splitting up in different directions as we emerge into the parking lot. Eddie, Gareth, Doug, and Jeff head toward their cars, while Mike, Lucas, and I wait near the doors for our ride—Nancy should be here any minute, having just finished up with an after-school newspaper meeting.

"Hey, this was really great," Mike says, voice tentative. "Are you guys doing anything now? Maybe we could persuade our parents to let us do a last-minute sleepover?"

I'm surprised, but pleasantly so. A few days ago, I wasn't sure I was even on speaking terms with my friends, and now it feels like we're stronger than we've been in a while. Not all the way better, maybe, but definitely *friends* again, which is what matters.

"That would be awesome," I say.

"Oh, maybe we can come to yours and you can finally show us your finished science project!" Mike says.

"You guys want to see the Bard Box?" I ask. Not bashfully, but a genuine question, because I don't want to bore them with it, but I'd love to show it off.

"Hell yes," Lucas says. "I wanna see what it can do, besides making fart noises."

"Yeah, and didn't you say Will made you art for the title?" Mike says. "You've gotta show us everything."

"Okay. I'm sure you guys can come over," I say, unable to contain my enthusiasm, so I end up bouncing on the balls of my feet.

My mom will complain about me not giving her advance notice, but that's not enough to deter me from doing it. *Sorry, Mom, and thank you.*

At the same time, though, the mention of the science project reminds me of my interview with Eastwood.

"Just, I have a call I need to make around five-thirty?" I

glance at them nervously and add, "My aunt Kathy. It's not a big deal. I'll just take it in another room."

"Yeah, sure," Mike says, just as Nancy pulls up and waves for us to get in her car.

I've been so on top of the world about Hellfire Club and Lucas joining that I've almost forgotten to be nervous about my interview. But honestly, with Mike and Lucas back by my side, I feel like I can handle anything.

▶

After Nancy drops us off at my house, we take turns calling our respective parents to make sure the sleepover is okay. Once that's settled, Mike and Lucas follow me up to my room to meet the Bard Box.

They've heard my presentation, but they haven't seen the poster board or heard the Bard Box's capabilities beyond the gags I harassed them with. So I demonstrate its abilities, but I get distracted talking about how Brian sabotaged the project and I had to improvise. I regale them with tales of "Crazy Train," and they're both so impressed and ask so many questions that I lose track of time.

Suddenly, I look at the clock and realize that it's five-thirty.

"Oh, crap," I say, thrusting the Bard Box into Mike's stomach. He lets out a little *oof* and grabs it from me. "I've gotta make a call, wait here!"

The last words are called over my shoulder as I sprint

out of my room and down the stairs, skidding to a stop in front of the phone.

But just as I grab Mr. Adams's business card, I notice a letter on the kitchen island that my mom must have brought in this morning. I recognize Will's familiar handwriting on the envelope. I pick it up.

I need to call. I *will* call, but the letter in my hands feels more important, so I put the call off for a minute or two more while I tear open the envelope and peel open the letter. Will's neat lines of writing fill the college-ruled paper.

I read:

Dec. 11, 1985

Dear Dustin,

The science fair sounds like it was quite the sweet adventure, wow! You're like the hero in a detective novel or something. And you were right, of course I adored Frodo Quackins. What a great name! It sounds like you had a great time. Thanks for telling me the whole tale.

As for the less fun stuff . . .

I'm going to be honest with you, it sounds like you and Lucas and Mike were <u>all</u> being jerks. I can only hope that by the time you get this letter, you've tried talking things out, but if you haven't: TALK TO THEM! COMMUNICATE! Our friends can be idiots, but they care about you. They care about the party. I really believe that.

I know what it's like to want things to be the way they used to be. The past year or so, I feel like that's all I've been doing. Wanting to play D&D with you guys, wanting to be back in Hawkins, wanting things to be _different._ But we can't go back to how things were. All we can do is move forward. And, I guess, hope that the people who matter are moving forward with us.

This new quest of yours . . . It sounds exciting, but (and maybe I'm reading too much into things?) you don't seem totally sold on it. Sure, you did awesome on your last solo quest. But there's a reason we're in a party. You can't do everything alone. You _don't have to_ do everything alone.

I think when it comes down to it, you'll make

the best choice for you. And when it comes down to it, I'm sure the party will be there for you, no matter what you choose.

I'll write soon with more updates from Lenora. For now, I just wanted to say congrats on the science fair, and I hope you (and Lucas and Mike) sort everything out soon.

Talk soon,

Will

At the bottom, there's an adorable doodle of a duck wearing a cloak and a necklace with a ring looped through it, and armed with a sword. I can only assume this is meant to be Frodo Quackins.

I huff a laugh through my nose, unable to hold back a smile even as I'm swallowing a lump in my throat. I hold the letter a beat longer than necessary, scanning the words again, before I set it down.

Because I have an interview to get to.

I pick up the phone and dial Mr. Adams. I'm only a few minutes late.

"Hi, this is Dustin," I say. "Sorry for the delay."

"Not a problem at all!" Mr. Adams says. "Is now still a good time to talk?"

"Yes," I say. "Yes, of course."

But Will's words are ringing in my head, mixing with Eddie's words from the other day, and Steve's, and my mom's, and I can barely focus on Mr. Adams introducing some important admissions woman and giving an introductory spiel about the school.

Because my mom is right, that it's a good opportunity. Steve is right, that I couldn't make this decision when I was angry at my friends. Eddie is right, that this would change things, my relationship with science, my relationship with my friends. And Will is right, that I can't go back, only forward.

"*. . . so with all of that said, we'd love to start the conversation by finding out why you're interested in coming to Eastwood,*" Mr. Adams says.

I hear Mike and Lucas break into boisterous laughter upstairs. I wonder what they're laughing about. I hate that I'm missing it.

"Yeah," I say.

Because that's the most basic question Mr. Adams could have asked. An essential question, to which I have dozens of answers prepared.

But none of them come to me. I'm blanking.

Or, I'm not blanking. I *know* the reasons.

I want to commit myself to science. I want to be surrounded by people who care about knowledge and curiosity. I want to make cool things, and ask cool questions, and find cool answers.

They're all good reasons, theoretically.

But they don't feel true anymore.

Or, they're true individually. But in response to the question *Why do I want to go to Eastwood?* I don't think they're true at all. They feel hollow. They feel like *excuses.*

I've *already* committed myself to science. I *have* friends who care about knowledge and curiosity. I've *made* cool things, asked cool questions, found cool answers. I don't need to go to Eastwood for that.

I think I wanted to have an escape route. I think I wanted a solution that felt easy, like a Band-Aid slapped over the problems with my friends. I think I was so afraid of getting left behind that I thought I'd leave first.

I think, maybe, I don't want to go to Eastwood at all.

*"Dustin?"* Mr. Adams asks. Because I've been silent for a long, long moment, and they're waiting for an answer.

*Why do I want to go to Eastwood?*

I *don't.* I don't want to be somewhere where someone can be so worried about a science fair that they'd sabotage projects to win. I don't want to be somewhere where even someone like Anika doesn't feel appreciated.

I want to be upstairs, with my friends, laughing at Mike's terrible Yoda impression or Lucas's attempts at karate moves that he's learned from magazines ever since Max said she thought the Karate Kid was hot. I want to be in Family Video, tearing up the new release section while Steve and Robin banter and give me a hard time for messing up their system. I want to be in Hellfire Club, helping Eddie spin stories of magic and heroes and adventure.

I want to be *here,* in Hawkins.

"I'm sorry," I say. "I appreciate your time—I'm really sorry. But I think—I think I have to go. I have somewhere else I need to be."

*"Oh,"* Mr. Adams says, disappointed. I don't care. I feel lighter than I have in weeks. *"I hope everything's okay. Do you want to reschedule for next week?"*

"No," I say. "No, I think—I'm good here, actually. I think I'm happy where I am."

There's a long beat of silence. A throat clearing.

*"Dustin,"* Mr. Adams says slowly, *"I really think you should consider this more carefully. It's a rare opportunity. We don't offer spots or scholarships to just anyone—"*

"I know," I say. "But I have a rare opportunity here in Hawkins, and I'd be an idiot to turn it down."

It's not even a lie. How can I turn down the chance to keep being myself, to keep loving science, to keep being with my best friends in the world for as long as I can? It's not just Mike and Lucas, but Max, too, and Steve, and Eddie.

Stunned silence stretches through the phone. I break it, happily.

"So, thank you for your time, but no thanks," I say, chipper. "Have a great weekend!"

And I hang up.

I bask in the silence of the kitchen for a long moment, staring down at Will's letter. I hear more laughter from upstairs. It beckons me like a siren's call, and I follow the sound up the stairs, down the hall, through the door of my bedroom.

"I'm not saying Frodo Quackins *isn't* an awesome name," Mike is saying. "I'm just saying there are other options."

"Okay, I'm listening," says Lucas.

"R2-Duck2," Mike says.

"No way," Lucas says.

"Emperor Quackatine?" Mike suggests. "Duck Vader? Or Duck Sidious?"

"What about Ducktor Who?" Lucas tries.

That sets them off into laughter again, and I hover in the doorway, watching, smiling. They're sitting on my bed with Bard Box between them, smiling for what seems like the first time in a long time. Mike notices my arrival and looks at me.

"Everything okay?" he asks.

I don't know if he's talking about the phone call, or something else entirely. Maybe I look insane, standing and smiling at them like an idiot. I don't care.

"Yeah," I say. "Yeah, everything's great."

A few minutes later, we're heading downstairs to the living room to watch *Gremlins.* Mike and Lucas get into a heated debate over who makes better microwave popcorn, while I point out that microwaving isn't exactly a skill. We gather a big enough pile of blankets to build a human-size nest, and the three of us pile onto the couch, sharing blankets and popcorn.

I'm sure Mike will talk through the movie like he always does, and I'm sure Lucas will fall asleep halfway through like *he* always does. When it's over, I'll probably complain about every plot hole just like *I* always do.

It's nice, sometimes, when things stay the same.

With Lucas and Mike on either side of me, the movie starts.

Really, there's no place I'd rather be.

# ACKNOWLEDGMENTS

I watched the first season of *Stranger Things* at age sixteen, when it came out as a little underdog show on Netflix, and I fell in love with it. I've watched every new season on release at midnight; I've written analysis; I've made gifsets; I've written fan fiction. I have loved this show with my whole heart over the course of eight years and counting, and I am so privileged and beyond lucky to have had the opportunity to write for a world I love so much.

I could spend ages waxing poetic about the following people, but I'll try to keep it quick:

Thank you to my amazing agent, John Cusick, for listening to me ramble obsessively about *Stranger Things* for an hour and, instead of thinking I'm a weirdo, setting out to get me the coolest job of my life.

Thank you to the team at Penguin Random House for bringing this book to life, but especially to my editor Geof Smith, for endless brainstorming and unwavering enthusiasm, and for putting trust in me as an author and as a fan.

Thank you to the *Stranger Things* and Netflix teams for making this project possible, and for giving me the amazing opportunity to play in this world and with this character. To the Duffer Brothers, for creating such an amazing and immersive world with so many lovable characters. To Paul Dichter, for providing essential insight and answering my many questions about Dustin and the world of *Stranger Things*.

Thank you to Gaten Matarazzo for bringing Dustin to life in such a vibrant way and making him the lovable nerd we have known and adored over the course of so many years.

Thank you to CL Montblanc, Christina Manolopoulos, and Jace Camedon for keeping me sane during a very intense drafting period. This book wouldn't exist without you guys, or at least, it would be a lot worse.

Finally, huge and immeasurable thanks to the passionate *Stranger Things* fandom for nourishing an amazing community of fans and for loving Dustin Henderson in all his nerdy glory. I hope this book made you love him even more. I know it did for me.